Bullet to Harm, Bullets to Heal

David Stewart Handelman

ISBN: 978-1-961169-40-1

Dedication

I wish to dedicate this book to my very patient wife, Judy, and, as always, to my children, Jeffrey, and Alisa.

As we travel through time, life has many obstacles we must overcome. We must always seek adventures that brighten our lives and, as always, push and reach for the stars.

Acknowledgment

I would like to acknowledge my wife, Judy, for having the patience to listen to me while I told her of the future of the book and where the main character was going.

Contents

About the Author

David Handelman was born in and remained in Chicago, Illinois, for many years, moving to Miami Beach and other states before taking a hard landing in the Los Angeles area. He started writing poems and other stories at 19 and continued to do the same for many years. Most of them were hidden, stored away in files, as he moved around the country looking for a home.

His life experiences are far too many to tell, attending different schools and having many jobs as he navigated through life. Finding solace in writing took him away from some of the complex realities surrounding him. He presently lives in the Los Angeles area with his wife.

Handelman is an accomplished author. His published works include *A New World of Selling Real Estate, Notes from a Quill*, *Between Spirit and Substance, The Assassin's Wife*, *The Gravel Road*, and *Sentiments*, a book of prose, poetry, and thoughts.

Other than poetry, he decided to indulge in this new novel, a sequel to "*The Gravel Road,*" which has been on his mind for many years.

Preface

It is said that the most unlikely situations, places, and backgrounds can yield the most unlikely friendships. Or better yet, in this case, situations surrounded by intrigue, mystery, blood, and bullets can yield friendships that can very well stand the test of time and geological borders.

Follow this second installment of the stories surrounding Jonah, who forms an unlikely alliance with Prince Najib, an art enthusiast who travels the world, collecting jewels, art, and property from the strangest places.

Najib and Jonah find themselves in a situation that could very well end this Prince's livelihood and his actual life along with it. They embark on a journey to discover who could be behind the heinous and malicious attacks on Jonah's friend, who has turned more into a brother.

Jonah uses his skills as a master auctioneer to discover the depths of a plot that goes far beyond the predictions of Najib, the Prince, and his colleagues, who are masters of the art of espionage and bullet plays. They discover how they can be targeted in new ways that not only keep them on their toes but also reveal that an assassin's work is never done.

Chapter 1: Time

"This will never happen to me, NEVER!" The then cold and bewildered child had come a long way. People tried to sympathize with him, but he was none other than Jonah Knight. He did not have time for sympathies and comments that were uncalled for. He knew he wanted a better life for himself, and he made sure to strive his way to get it. He had built himself into a man who was known for his name and power.

According to people, Jonah wanted the money and was always after it. However, that was not the case, at least not entirely. Jonah knew the life he chose for himself came with a cost, but the power it brought to his name was real.

In a situation such as this, a person has two options, either sulk over the past and make your life miserable or become fearless and run after what you want. Jonah opted for the latter, and it served him well.

He learned to live with a rock-solid exterior to fool the world because he had gravely realized the depth of Flagstaff's words. But, in the darkness of the night, the young man in the picture was still the same Jonah who worked hard to become the man he was today.

***

Liquor, smoke, beer, unique dishes- the redolence filled the air of the pub. People sat in different groups as waves of laughter echoed in the obvious corners.

The bartenders seemed to be having one of those sloppy drip trip days, serving one table after the other. The vibe there screamed the words 'chatty,' 'chaotic,' and 'slightly tipsy.' However, the chill atmosphere lasted only a few hours before the glass of the windows came crashing down to the floor.

The still of the early evening was overpowered by the sound of the shattering glass when three bullets smashed through the window at Oliver's Tavern.

"EVERYBODY! HIT THE FLOOR, NOW!" The bartender covered his ears with both of his hands and was yelling at the top of his lungs while everyone was panicking.

Earlier, Jonah was seen walking into Oliver's Tavern in Hays, Kansas. He, too, sat down under the table, pushing his body toward the floor. *"Guess not all of my enemies are dead,"* he sarcastically mumbled to himself as his mouth formed a side smirk.

"What was that?" an unknown man manically screamed, questioning everyone around him. When he noticed that everyone was too involved in the situation to even care about answering him, he shouted yet again, *"Will someone say something? What was that?"*

"It is probably a hunter checking his gun, and it mistakenly went off. Luckily, no one was hurt," the bartender replied, but Jonah knew better. He knew the circumstances that usually led to open fire.

It had been over a year; Jonah had not been contacted by anyone for anything except for a few local auctions. The gift of peacefulness that he had been experiencing was certainly welcomed after countless years of running, being shot at, and tortured by his enemies. When Jonah returned to his seat, his mind could not help but wander back to the past years, or at least the last two. It was a conflict that involved blood, trauma, and unraveled truths. They thought they could break him, but he knew how to fight and come back stronger than ever. Jonah was raised in the midst of chaos; nobody else knew how to deal with it better than he did.

He had seen and observed more than what children his age could even begin to fathom. After all these years, Jonah had grown up to be a strong-minded individual. He knew every situation had a breakthrough; it took a focused pair of eyes to find it, though. This was why he had to be focused and confident about his surroundings every passing second.

In a world where children of his age grew under the shower of their parents' love and affection, Jonah was alone and determined to face the ugly side of it at a young age—a side only twisted and warped adults were aware of.

But in Jonah's case, he wanted to get involved. Then he did it. He stepped into that hideous part of society. Somehow, he managed to pave his way to greatness on this side as well.

If anyone were to observe him, they would not be able to tell that he was a newbie in this sector. The confidence he walked with made people fear him. He had a silent exterior, one that he was taught to maintain besides always being aware of his surroundings.

Jonah understood business which was why he was the best at what he did. People around the globe knew his name. Some wanted him to get their work done, some were after him, while some just admired him for the man he was. After the traumatic events that had taken place, he chose to strengthen himself and not let anything else ever affect him.

He depended on his parents, and what did he get? *Nothing.* Just because the hours of desperation were too much for his parents to handle, they opted to leave him all alone.

Not even once, though, did they think about how Jonah, an eight-year-old, would survive the graveness of this universe when they couldn't. It was an ongoing, vicious cycle; he was running from his past while his past kept sprinting back to him.

The sound of the gunshots had awakened the horror of the night as he watched his world fall apart. Every time he was reminded of that night, the same years old coldness and numbness took over his being. He would stare into thin air with a longing look in his eyes. The fact that he had not given up, unlike his parents, was not a surprise to anyone.

He was one incomparable man who believed in dealing with his problems rather than running away from them. He was not a coward; he had made a mark in the same place where he was left alone. Jonah was a man of little words and more actions.

If it were anyone else in the same position as his, they would not have come this far. Although there were times when he could not help but sit and knock around on the roads of his unusual past, he no longer lived in it.

He had worked hard to get where he was today. He knew the man he had become and was proud of himself. Under no circumstances would he let anyone, or anything take that away from him- *not even his past.*

Every gunshot reminded him of the night his father shot himself. He didn't know what a gunshot sounded like until that very night. Thanks to his father, he was fully familiar with the sound now. After his father's death, he had hoped to find solace in his mother's lap, only to discover that she, too, had left him all alone.

For now, he only yearned for a place to call home and a family. He craved a family to come home to. A house filled with love and laughter of his miniature versions. Randomly sitting in his backyard with his wife along with a cup of coffee or weekly runs to the ice cream parlor with the kids; he wanted it all. He craved a family as he had never known one. After all the things he was put through, he knew he deserved a happily ever after, even if it came with a price. Although Jonah had been on the run for almost a year now, he knew people were still after his blood.

When Jonah returned to his seat, his mind was fully occupied with random thoughts, sliding in one after the other. He had not heard from his good friend, Prince Najib, or any of his other friends.

The government agents that kept threatening him were nowhere to be found. His friendship with the Prince was not a long one, but it had lasted long enough to show him that he genuinely cared about Jonah.

It started when Jonah saved Najib's life. It was at that moment the Prince knew that he would forever be indebted to Jonah for his heroic action. It was not every day that a person would sprint in to save someone else's life with no regard for their own.

Although the Prince had only known Jonah personally for a short period of time, the love they shared for each other's company made him consider Jonah as a brother.

Upon his first meeting with the Prince, Jonah found out that the Prince had known Flagstaff, who was a good friend of the Prince's father growing up.

Peter Flagstaff was a father figure to Jonah. He made him what he was; he was the push Jonah desperately needed to become something in life. Then Jonah discovered that Peter was admired by the Prince and his father as well. Jonah instantly knew his friendship with the Prince would last long because of their partnership.

Jonah was convinced that no other person had the skills to become his great friend in such a short period of time. Part of the reason why their friendship transformed and took another level instantly was because they had become very fond of each other.

This was why the Prince still had not contacted him even once was kind of worrying for Jonah. A number of thoughts crowded his mind, *"Did I do something to offend him? Has something happened to him? I wonder why he was trying so hard to save me...."*

"Hello Jonah, how are you, my man?" Jonah's thoughts were interrupted by a familiar face.

Chapter 2: Unrequited

A young man in well-fitted blue jeans and a grey-colored T-shirt named Brett appeared in front of Jonah. He had an oval face with brushed-up hair. Although he was in his mid-twenties, his full beard made him look years older than his actual age. His words were loud enough to pull Jonah out of his thoughts.

"Hey! Wassup, Brett? I'm good," Jonah said while trying his best to appear as calm as possible to not look like he was busy thinking about his work yet again.

Brett was one of the boys from town who had been after Jonah since his return. Every time he saw Jonah, he would come to him in the hopes of becoming his close friend. However, Jonah was aware of his intentions, so he kept his distance.

"Yeah, yeah, man, I'm alright. Just trying to live life right like ya," Brett said as he chuckled.

"Ha-ha..." Jonah scoffed and shifted his attention back to his basic martini cocktail. Every guy in town treated Jonah with the utmost respect, but only he knew the reason behind all these happy greetings.

Everyone was after Jonah and his knowledge to persuade others. Jonah's name was the most heard and wanted on the streets. Even his distant observers knew that if they went to him with their requirements, he would meet their expectations. Jonah was an expensive man, but that, too, because he knew the work, he offered was extraordinary.

The man understood that Jonah was in no mood to chat with him at that moment and took his leave soon after.

The short interaction with that young man was just another example of what used to happen in Jonah's life. Everyone in town had a different image of Jonah painted in their minds. People assumed that he had the dream life of every living being on the planet. The older adults praised him for the work he had been doing for the town, while the youngsters couldn't help but want to get closer to him because of his lavish charisma.

Quiet, confident, and tenebrous were the words people used to describe Jonah. Every move he made attracted a new bunch of audience. There was a time when he was a child, and everyone felt bad for him. To think that the same child had grown into this self-reliant adult was why people regarded him well.

All of them thought that he spent his days touring the world and that he was on vacation every other month. But not even a single soul was aware of what went on behind the closed doors of his life.

No one in Hays, Kansas, knew anything about the life he had secretly built from scratch and the unlimited amount of hard work it took. Nobody knew that he was associated with half of the most dangerous people in the world. That he not only worked with them, but he was also on the way to becoming one of them.

He knew that even if he wanted to, he wouldn't let anyone into his happening life. But when he watched people come after him thinking he was living an ideal life, it made him want to scoff right in front of their faces. Beyond any doubt, his life was a rollercoaster filled with thrill.

Jonah had become so sly and good at hiding his actual life that nobody could even imagine the events that were taking place. Whenever he left the town, people automatically assumed that he was far away on vacation.

On the flip side, Jonah closed himself inside the four walls because sometimes, even strong people like him couldn't bear the burden of their own thoughts. *"Alexis..."* The one name that popped up in his mind often. Every time he thought of her, he was hit with a new string of pain.

Jonah was in love with her. He could feel himself thinking more and more about her with every passing day. It might not have been the same for Alexis. However, for Jonah, Alexis was slowly becoming the center of his attention. Even though it lasted for a short period, their time together was filled with bright-lit sun, waves of continuous glee, and days and nights full of love.

Just getting to be with her and spending time with her was enough. Why would he want anything else? She had become the reason for most of his smiles. Although Jonah was very secretive about his life, he often dreamed of meeting someone with whom he could share all aspects and secrets of his life. But not all of them – he remembered what Flagstaff had told him, *"Trust no one."*

He was very careful, always on high alert. But Alexis had found Jonah's soft side. He usually woke up at night and stared at Alexis's petite figure, peacefully sleeping on the other side of the bed.

He would draw her closer to his body until her back was flush with his chest. He often put his arm around her and snuck closer into the warmth of her skin. Taking in her scent as he would be reminded of the fact that, finally, it was his turn to look forward to life.

Time after time, he thought to himself that after years of yearning for affection and love, his gravel road was coming to an end. He thought that with Alexis beside him, he was no longer alone. It was Jonah and Alexis against the world. Little did Jonah know, not all of his dreams would turn into a reality. It took him hardly a few days to fall for her.

"Only if you had not played this game with me. I would have fought the world just to keep you with me. I wonder if she actually loved me... How can you love someone so much and, on the other hand, not even care about them?"

Jonah sighed as the thoughts in his mind had taken an unexpected turn, "*She pretended to love me only so she could stay close to me.*" Jonah's heart was having a hard time accepting what his mind had already understood.

Although it had been over a year, some parts of Jonah still missed Alexis terribly. She was the only person he thought was suitable for him after all the years of trauma. She was no longer with him, but his heart frequently thought about her.

"*She had to die, or else I wouldn't have lived...*" Jonah reminded himself. He still missed the peace she brought him in the darkness of night when the world seemed to be far away from him.

Like every other stage of life, this, too, was a test he had to pass, and Jonah knew how to ace every exam. Jonah's personality required him to let go of things once they were out of his life.

Chapter 3: Trouble Comes Knocking

A few weeks later, when the thoughts in his head became a little too much to handle, Jonah decided to visit the site where it all had begun; his home and the farm his family once owned in Hays, Kansas. The sky was as dark as his thoughts, but the stars shone everywhere, indicating that the best was yet to come.

The middle of nowhere was the center of all the trauma that he had seen. At the end of the gravel road was the house where it all started. As soon as he drove down to the place, he once called home, everything flashed before his eyes—the death of both his parents, Peter Flagstaff, his mentor, and the house at the end of Gopher Street. His grip tightened on the door as he stepped out of the car.

The air there was still as cold as that night. The scenes from that specific night came running back to his mind when his eyes darted over to the tree where his mother hung herself. Then he remembered his father lying on the barn floor, bloody, with pieces of flesh sprayed out of his head.

Jonah stood far away from the farm beside his car. His eyes never moved as he kept staring at the tree and the old barn when the new owner of the once Knight farm approached, *"Hey, can I help you with something?"*

Jonah flinched and turned around, *"Ahh, no, no.... I was just looking around. I used to live here as a kid,"* Jonah replied.

"You must be the Knight kid, huh? All grown-up you are!" The old man added.

"Yep, that's me!"

"You are doing a great job with the farm, and it looks terrific. Keep it up! Not everyone has the guts to do so much with such little time." Jonah nodded his head and turned around to head back to his Pontiac Sedan.

"Thanks for coming. I hope I get to see you again. Before you leave, though, would you like a cup of coffee with the wife?" The old man said, giving Jonah a warm smile.

"Nope, gotta go. Maybe next time!" And with that, Jonah drove off quickly down the road. The sound of the loose gravel road hitting the underside of the car was all too familiar.

Before Jonah had left for his various life-threatening adventures overseas, he had provided enough money to have the whole house maintained well because he wasn't sure when he would return or if he would ever get the chance to come back.

Jonah had placed twenty-five thousand dollars at the Hays National Bank. He had saved them in there for the maintenance of his home, for any repairs, and for the basic upkeep of the house.

Even though he did not like Tyrone Rhodes, the President of the bank, he knew he could trust the bank with his money because he was an honest man.

Although he had been hoping to step out of this business for a long time, he knew it was not that easy. He remembered Flagstaff told him that in this business, once you are in, it is not easy to get out.

They will either put you on the grounds of a dangerous auction or try to kill you. *"Always watch your back,"* Flagstaff said, *"Trust no one."* He was always on high alert because he knew anything could happen; time and place didn't matter. He was aware of the price he would have to pay when he decided to get in, and now, he was ready to get out of it.

***

Although the streets were glowing with bright city lights, the stars filled the sky. It looked like sugar was spilled over black marble. It was the promise of life in darkness. A sense of warmth was springing from the cold. It was a vastness to bring humbleness and infinite space to bring gratitude for the coziness of home. No matter the number of years that passed, Jonah saw each night sky as a fresh gift given anew.

Jonah found himself staring up at the blanket of stars that stretched to no limits until the occasional barking of faraway dogs broke his stance, making him continue his walk down the street.

He had just gotten done with an extravagant dinner at Margie's. Margie's was known to be one of the most affordable diners in town. They had delicious food and offered a greater quantity which was why on some busy nights, Jonah preferred to eat there.

As he walked on the footpath, he couldn't help but ponder upon the fact that the last year had been different from many other years of his life. *Bullets, weapons, darkness, and blood*- this was how he had spent many years of his life. The fact that the previous year had been rather calm with no involvement of blood or bullets surprised him but also made him happy.

Nonetheless, Jonah remained one of the most feared individuals in town. There was no doubt that people came to him to ask for help, but that didn't change the fact that nobody had the guts to question him. Although Jonah's mind was occupied with many unraveling thoughts, his senses were still on high alert. No matter where he was or what he was busy doing, his job required him to be on his toes at all times.

A thudding noise of tires and a screeching sound from under the hood caught his attention. Jonah knew giving a sudden reaction would make things suspicious from his side, so he kept walking in a calm manner.

The brake pad hit the rotor, causing Jonah to hear the squeaking sound. Slowly and sharply, the driver stopped the car right beside Jonah. He realized in a moment that whoever was inside knew very well that Jonah wouldn't be able to do anything considering the circumstance, which was why they had approached him at that hour.

A black Citroen Berlingo stood in front of Jonah. *"1.5 BlueHDi, 1000 kg, Enterprise 130ps, and short wheelbase,"* he stared through the tinted passenger window. *"Nice van,"* he said, showcasing his strength that even during the worst of situations, he was not scared of anyone.

However, Jonah knew that he wouldn't be able to resist. This was why as soon as the van's door slid open with a command to get in, he hopped inside without uttering a word.

At this point, Jonah wondered whether this was for an auction or if he had jumped inside the lion's den. Usually, this was exactly how people approached him when they were looking for his help as an auctioneer.

At first, there was barely any light, and the tinted windows made Jonah's surroundings darker than they already were. Jonah had made up his mind that they were about to take him somewhere, but the car seemed to stay motionless. That was when the two men who were sitting in the front seats turned around and eyed Jonah head to toe.

Both men were dressed in black suits; the only difference was that one of them was wearing a green and orange floral Aloha shirt instead of a white-collar shirt underneath his coat. Jonah stared at him with one raised brow, analyzing his questionable taste.

It looked as if the guy in the Aloha shirt had dressed up for an upcoming beach party. *"What? Why are you looking at me like that?"* the guy asked.

Without flinching, Jonah kept staring at him, indicating that he was interested in nothing else other than finding out why he was there.

"Well, my name is Jim, and this is Larry," Jim said, pointing toward the man sitting in the driver's seat. It was then that Jonah realized the van had started moving.

Quietly, Jonah kept staring at Jim, who was now talking as if everything was normal, and they had not just picked up Jonah without his consent and any logical explanation.

Jonah zoned out, thinking about all the times this had happened in the past few years. Every time, some random car would stop him in his tracks and then pull him inside as if this act was totally normal.

But then again, this side of the world required such a level of secrecy. If every matter were eligible to be discussed in the open air, a lot of their secret missions would have been aborted.

On this side, though, every being had two faces; one that they displayed in front of the whole world and the other that remained hidden no matter the circumstances.

So did Jonah; what he was and what he wasn't continued to be a confusing question. His life had turned out in such a way that it took him only a few months to discover the opposite personalities that he needed to ace in this business. Living with Flagstaff only helped his situation gravitate more deeply and transformed it into Jonah's reality.

Soon after, Jonah became known for his twisted ways and sharp mind in the business world. Although there was a huge number of people who claimed to know Jonah, there was merely a handful who actually knew him. Because they had seen him working or they got the chance to talk to him related to work, they assumed that they knew the real 'Jonah Knight.'

However, they were wrong because one of the many things that Flagstaff taught him was, *"Never let anyone know all about you,"* which indeed turned out to be a very helpful piece of advice throughout Jonah's career.

"You get it now, man?" Jim's question brought Jonah back to his continuous blabbering.

"What does that mean?" Jonah asked, shifting his gaze from Larry to Jim, *"and what am I supposed to do?"*

Jonah's strong exterior and uninterested face reflected that he would listen to their blabbering for only so long now. Jim had heard about Jonah, the mystery man, before. He knew that Jonah was the best in the business and never bowed down to anyone's unnecessary virtue, which was why Jim and Larry were warned that they had to make this work.

Jim took a long and heavy breath before answering Jonah's question, *"You remember the diamonds you sold for the Prince?"*

"What about it?" Jonah answered, he had a feeling that this was about to push him into a pit of obstacles.

"You have affronted and outraged an extremely important person by selling those diamonds to the wrong bidder. He wanted those diamonds, and you ended up selling them to someone else," Jim answered, shaking his head.

"Your guy must not have made a higher bid, or else I would have sold it to him," Jonah said peacefully.

Larry was about to take the gun out of his shin band, but Jim immediately put his hand on Larry's to stop him. Jim then turned to Jonah with a menacing smile and said, *"You will have to listen to us anyway and do exactly what we tell you to do. We know you are friends with Najib, which is why we will use your friendship to find him."*

Jonah laughed and stated, *"It has been a year since I last talked to him. I have no idea about his whereabouts or-"*

Jim smiled sarcastically and cut off Jonah, *"My man, you won't have to wait much as the Prince himself will contact you soon for an important auction. All we want is for you to lead us to the Prince. We will take care of the rest."*

Jonah leaned in toward Jim with his hands wrapped together and was about to refuse to be part of their envious plan when Jim turned toward Jonah with a smile – it was a smile that promised a blood war, full of promising threats.

Unexpectedly, Larry slammed the brakes, which led to the van stopping in a sudden motion. Jonah would have been thrown to the front part of the van, but he gripped the seat tightly and kept his composed posture.

They dropped off Jonah at his doorstep and hurriedly vanished into thin air. Jonah entered his house and then his office, slumped on his chair, and dawned upon the mess he had been sucked into. He knew that this was the end of the pit for him; he knew that there was no way out of this situation. He had no contact with the Prince, or he would have told him each and every detail right this very second. Jonah was stuck between the harsh reality that had forced him into having a constant quarrel in his mind.

Chapter 4: Chipped

The night sky looked picturesque through the single-hung window in Jonah's bedroom. The backdrop of the full moon was a navy-shaded black. The night sky was so clear that almost every star cluster was visible to the eye. A glowing yellowy white reflecting from the moon was surrounded by an ethereal glow, and millions of stars were sprinkled behind it.

But the peaceful night sky contradicted Jonah's chaotic state of mind; it was proof that sometimes, even the calming nature could not prevent the bitterness of reality in a person's life.

Jonah's mind had been in a state of constant disarray since the last night. After many long years, he had made a genuine friend, the Prince, whom he kept in extremely high regard. Jonah could not even imagine something happening to him, so to think that he was the one leading all those dangerous people to the Prince was unthinkable.

Jonah kept reminding himself that he would find a way out of this, even though part of him was well aware of the fact that that was not possible, especially with everything that had happened last night. Although the Prince had not contacted Jonah for over a year, Jonah's friendship with the Prince remained very close to his heart.

They understood each other and the lives they were living. Despite being in entirely opposite businesses, both led almost the same life, filled with people who were running after them, a requirement to be on their toes and to stay alert of their surroundings at all times.

Jonah seemed to find no resolution for the problem at hand; he needed to gain a greater perspective, take a step back with a deep breath, and see the wide-angle version to figure out how to reach the Prince.

Hours were spent in agony and confusion before Jonah had finally fallen asleep, only to wake up to the unstoppable ringing sound of his office phone. An irritated, worried, and groggy Jonah stepped into his office, walked toward the desk, and answered the constantly ringing phone.

A familiar voice jolted his eyes wide open on the other end of the line. With a raised brow, after recognizing the voice of his old friend, he asked, *"Abdul?"*

"A car will be there to pick you up at eight sharp. Be ready! You know how this works," Abdul responded without paying much heed to Jonah's surprising yet questioning tone.

Jonah wanted to tell him what had happened last night, but he knew he was being watched, and one wrong move would cost him his life. He could feel the eyes of all those who were hungry and after his power all around him. This was one of the advantages of being in this business; Jonah had learned to always keep his senses on high alert. On the other hand, Abdul didn't even care to hold the call for a good two seconds.

"I could have tried to drop some hints," Jonah mumbled to himself and put the receiver back on the cradle.

It wasn't Abdul's fault; that was how the system worked. No extra words were shared, every sentence was supposed to be to the point, and that was supposed to be the end of the discussion. There wasn't much Jonah could have done either, and that was why he was more exasperated than ever. He had been involved in this business for years now, all while acing every step. He was used to being in control of situations around him; he had that kind of power. However, at that very moment, his enragement was taking a hit because he badly wanted to help his dear friend and couldn't find a way to do it.

Occupied in his thoughts, Jonah put the receiver down, still thinking about the dots that he could connect to escape the situation that had unfolded itself before him. Merely a second had passed when his doorbell started ringing.

Jonah walked back to the main door and peeked through the peephole, only to find Jim standing there with folded arms and a creepy smile glued to his face. Jim patiently stood in the same position waiting for Jonah to open the door as if it was very normal for him to visit him in the middle of the night. *"What's up with him and his weird choice of clothes?"* Jonah thought to himself. Yet again, Jim was wearing a blue and yellow Hawaiian beach T-shirt with yellow jeans and a pair of white sneakers.

Peeking through the peephole, Jonah sighed as it became abundantly clear to him that he wouldn't be able to run away or hide – which wasn't a part of his valiant nature anyway. But he knew that if he had gotten the option to disappear this time, he would have done it for the sake of his dear friend's life. However, Jonah realized it wasn't possible when he saw more than two black V8s filled with men empty out in front of his main door.

Somewhere in his mind, Jonah was still contemplating whether or not he could put up a fight. But given the circumstances, Jonah knew he would die fighting, and as much as he loved thrilling adventures, he had never planned on dying like this.

Jonah shook his head and, with a straight face, turned the knob, and opened the door to a smiling Jim. He then took a brief overview of all the men standing around his house and questioned Jim, *"How may I help you at this hour?"*

"Well, can't leave you alone until we are completely done with you, you know?" Jim responded to Jonah's question.

"What more do you want?" Jonah asked, showcasing from his words that he was annoyed at this point.

"We haven't even started doing anything, Jonah, my man!" Jim said, masking his evil smile. *"And we don't want much, honestly; we just want you to take us to the Prince, remember?"*

"I know," Jonah replied in a stern tone. *"Can I get more details on the guy who has asked you to do all this? After all, I'm helping you all!"* Jonah added.

"That and all the other details will only be revealed once we are done with our task, can't trust anyone in this business now, ain't I right, Jonah?" Jim responded to Jonah's question.

"Of course!" Jonah said as he glared at Jim and all the men around him, making sure each and every one of them knew he was not afraid of anyone.

"So, what did they say?" Jim asked, spinning the conversation back to the main topic.

"Who? Said what?" Jonah questioned, covering his tone with confusion, pretending as if Abdul hadn't just called him.

"You know what, Jonah, I'm going to give you some advice," Jim started his sentence as he slowly circled around Jonah, *"never lie to people who have been after you – watching every move of yours closely, because then all hell breaks loose!"*

As soon as those words left Jim's mouth, he gave Jonah a small side smile and gestured his men to come forward and do whatever it was that they were here to do to him. Two big men, wearing black skin-tight t-shirts that revealed their fighter arms with camo trousers and black soldier boots, came forward. Every step they took made a loud thumping noise on the floor of Jonah's house.

"Comply with us, or things will definitely start getting much more painful, you get it?" Jim stated a double-meaning sentence, and Jonah understood the depth of his words.

Not even seconds later, the two men gripped Jonah's shoulders from both sides while a woman came in walking, moved to Jonah's side, and implanted something deep into his skin.

Jonah resisted for a while, but it was not long after that he felt the sharpness of a blade that had cut through his flesh and then meddled somewhere inside his arm. It was too late now. Whatever the woman had inserted into his skin had embedded itself in his bone.

After a while, Jim left with his men. Jonah was still unsure of their departure; he was skeptical that some of them were still hiding somewhere outside his house to make sure he wouldn't run away. Heading toward his bedroom, Jonah turned his body to face the full-length mirror. He caressed his arm where the installation had been done.

Although Jonah's subconscious mind understood what had just happened, his conscious mind couldn't process it.

There was a fog in his mind that he needed to immediately clear because he knew that things would only fall apart from this moment onward.

He could feel his bones cracking and thudding every time he made a slight movement with his left arm. It didn't hurt as much as it caused irritation in the depths of his bone. Overall, Jonah looked untouched and perfectly alright, but his heart and mind were still set on the words Jim had uttered before leaving his place, *"This chip inside you will help us keep an eye on you, and most importantly, this will make you help us get to the man we have been running after. Don't worry, though; it is just a chip, and you won't be harmed in any way! Just take us to your friend; that's all we ask of you!"* With that, Jim winked at Jonah and left with a sly smile pasted on his face.

Chapter 5: The Prince

Small flickers of lightning could be seen, which was a surprise to everyone as the weather forecast had not shown any signs of sudden changes. But changes never come with an application in advance; they simply invade the place they want to– exactly like in Jonah's life.

Jonah's ride to the destination was calm and quick. Like Abdul had instructed, a car was outside Jonah's house at eight sharp. When the driver announced that they had reached their destination, Jonah hesitated before opening the door, not because he was scared for himself, but because he was scared for his friend.

He took a deep breath, adjusted the expression on his face back to an unreadable one, and got off the car. Jonah looked around, still trying his level best to come up with a solution to the problem that was about to change his life all over again.

It was then Jonah spotted Najib, his dear friend. The Prince was standing at the foot of the private jet, at a very short distance from him. While he was walking toward his old friend, Jonah couldn't stop his mind from thinking about the fact that he was leading murderers to his dear friend, but he couldn't do anything about it.

In any other situation, Jonah would have jumped into the middle of the chaos and saved his friend's life because that was his nature. He didn't fear anybody, and everyone was aware of that, which was why these people had used him as bait to get to the Prince. Jonah wanted to do something, he wanted to fight everyone who was following them and warn Najib, but he knew – he understood that both of them could be pushed toward death because of his one wrong move. He wasn't entirely in the wrong; only if Najib had kept a source through which Jonah could contact him at times like these, things would have been different.

His walk toward Najib was nothing but filled with remorse and anxiety, his brain working at full capacity to come up with a solution. With every step Jonah took that got him closer to Najib, the anxiety shot up into his being and had successfully traveled to his eyes now.

Jonah tried to maintain his stubborn, stern, and unaffected gaze, but his eyes betrayed him and instead showcased terror. Najib, who had been observing Jonah's hesitation for a few seconds, now understood the look in Jonah's eyes. In a rapid motion, Najib turned around to alert security.

The moment Najib turned around to gesture to the security, shots rang out. The loud screeching sound of the wheels filled the air. Jonah covered his ears as the sound of the gunshots and screeching wheels got louder every passing second amidst the sandstorm that was created by the many vehicles that were drifting, speeding, and hastily driving toward them.

The entire situation felt as if it was a scene from a movie. Like in any movie, the goons ran toward the one man they had been after their whole life while the man tried his best to escape their wrath until his last breath. The cars that were speeding toward Najib and Jonah looked like hungry, wild animals running after their prey.

Jonah's thoughts were disturbed when he got pulled into a bullet-proof four-wheeler vehicle. He was shocked when he witnessed the intensity of preparation of his rivals, *"they really want him dead..."* Jonah mumbled to himself.

He turned around to look at the man sitting before him, only to realize it was none other than the Prince himself. At that moment, all he was grateful for was that the Prince was alright. Continuous shots were being fired at the Prince's car, but since it was a bullet-proof vehicle, Jonah was able to breathe in peace. However, nothing could change the fact that Jonah was still surprised about how quickly Najib, the Prince, reacted. It almost seemed as if Najib knew something like this would happen. Jonah was aware that the Prince's mind worked as fast as his, which was why he was able to detect the warning just by looking at Jonah's face. Najib did not wait for a second to stop and ask, mostly because he knew Jonah. Najib was attentive to the constant stern and unreadable look on Jonah's face every time they met. This was why he took immediate action when he noticed that Jonah's expressions were totally different.

As the car started to drive away from the chaos, Jonah didn't care to take longer than two seconds to catch a well-awaited breath and immediately jumped onto the point. He looked straight at Najib and, with penetrating concentration, told him every bit of detail about the previous night.

"I was randomly stopped by two men who asked me to lead them to you. They said that I had made a mistake by selling the diamonds to the wrong bidder, and now there would be consequences. I kept insisting that we hadn't had any contact in the past year, but they did not believe me. They mentioned that I would get a call from you for some kind of auction, and at first, I thought they were bluffing because how would they know?

Jonah shook his head side-to-side, exhaling air from his nose, and continued, "*But I was wrong. They knew a lot more than I could have imagined. The second Abdul called to inform me about the car, I thought of telling him, but I knew one wrong move could have changed my life forever. If we had been in any kind of contact, I would have reversed the scenario and attacked them instead.*"

Najib presented an understanding nod and said, "*But we are safe now. I know a place; they won't be able to find us there.*"

"But I..." Jonah tried to speak when Najib cut him off and said, *"Trust me. I, too, have been in this business for a long time now. So I know how to deal with such people. All my life, I protected my precious belongings and ran miles to save them, and now, you can say I'm skillful enough to escape as many tough situations as I want."*

"That's not the thing," Jonah stated, *"they will follow us, Najib. They chipped me; they knew that you would be smart enough to sense the danger. I'm the one who brought them here, and even though that was not my intention at all, I'm the one who should be left behind. You should leave me with them and save your life. I know myself; I will fight through and might even come back."*

Najib's expression quickly transformed as he let out a small laugh. Suddenly, Najib didn't feel like his usual self to Jonah. Instead, his face now showcased a sly smile as he wore a cunning expression. This was the Najib everyone was after. In a solemn, powerful accent, Najib confidently spoke, *"You will be taken care of."*

At that moment, Jonah felt like his time had come. All the memories of his life flashed right before his eyes as he started believing that those moments would be his last. He was convinced the Prince would have him killed for leading murderers to him.

The car suddenly stopped as Jonah jolted in his place. He looked around and saw that it had stopped in the middle of nowhere. *"This is it,"* he muttered to himself as if those were his last moments.

Unexpectedly, the heavy and loud gushes of wind indicated that something odd was happening. Jonah looked out of the window and saw a helicopter getting ready to take-off.

"Go, go, go!" Najib shouted as he gestured for Jonah to climb onto the chopper. Confused, Jonah stepped toward it and, as he turned to look at the Prince, he saw that Najib had already left in his car.

Chapter 6: Headquarters

Jonah hurriedly climbed aboard the helicopter with some help and sat in one of the passenger seats of the helicopter, the very same helicopter Najib had gestured to after the bullet shower. As Jonah stepped into the helicopter, he was first told to buckle up by the man seated next to him, and when he saw what was in the man's hand, one thing became exceedingly clear—wherever he was being flown to would be a private location. Najib's associates immediately blindfolded him but kept him seated properly like a guest. They did not treat him like a hostage.

Jonah instantly understood that the helicopter's destination and the journey would be undisclosed. The destination was so secretive and secure that the Prince did not even consider Jonah privy to the information. But at the same time, he understood this was part of the job and that there would not always be information they both shared. No matter how many life-or-death situations they went through together, the underlying fact was that this was always going to be the nature of their business.

Jonah was brilliant, though. By the distance they were traveling inside the helicopter, he could tell that they were now well past the city's borders. They were either going to kill him or take him somewhere secure by his intuition. Either way, he could think of just one word to mumble under his breath. *"Shit...."*

Jonah knew that whenever someone was in a hostage situation similar to his, the trick was to avoid panicking at all costs. He knew that he had gathered all his courage to remain calm and not show an ounce of fear through his body language. He could think of one silver lining, however.

His eyes were covered with a blindfold. This was a good thing since his eyes were usually always the first to give away any emotion bubbling under the surface.

Even though he was well equipped with methods to disarm his current handlers, he knew there was a time and place for every technique. Jonah was aware of the fact that he was outnumbered inside that tiny metal cage, and things could quickly go sideways if he tried anything clever. Then suddenly, Jonah could sense the helicopter reducing its pace. The speed of the wings was slowing down, and the seats beside him had their passengers fiddling with their seatbelts. He then felt the thud of the helicopter when it touched the ground.

Jonah could hear someone pick up some bags while another one of Najib's subordinates guided him gently to exit the helicopter.

As soon as Jonah got off the chopper's ladder, he felt concrete beneath his feet. They were at some sort of a building, but no matter how much he racked his brain, Jonah couldn't think of any facility or building outside of the city. As far as he knew, mountains covered the entire region in the outskirts. The air was colder than the city's atmosphere, making him utterly confident that they were somewhere in the middle of the mountains. But a building? In the mountains? He couldn't figure that part out. But that was soon going to be answered.

As soon as Najib's subordinates got Jonah inside, they took his blindfold off. Jonah didn't say anything; he simply observed all around where he stood. He took in every detail of the area and made sure he could identify the exits. The area looked like a facility for experimentation on animals or maybe even humans; *who knew*? The iron-clad walls, painted white, were as tall as an airplane hangar. The sterile and symmetrical appearance made the facility look like a makeshift laboratory and cage. The entire perimeter of the facility looked to be heavily guarded, from the giant main doors, the corners of the floor, and the narrow galleys above. Guards were roaming all around the area.

The severe security detail gave Jonah the impression that the secrecy of this facility was of the utmost priority. If Jonah didn't know any better, he would have considered the area a holding ground for dangerous experiments on close inspection. But who knows? Maybe it was a secret lab where groundbreaking research was being carried out for drug lords, or perhaps this was Area 51? But alas, there were no aliens in sight. Jonah contemplated the true purpose of this facility, as it was in the middle of the mountains, in a secure location, and hidden from the city.

Meanwhile, a woman donning a lab coat made her way to Jonah and gestured to take his jacket. By the look of this woman, Jonah realized Najib knew what he was doing because he recognized that the only way to ease Jonah into the swing of things and help him was to incorporate the assistance of an attractive female. Jonah was a professional when it came to his job and the duties he was required to fulfill, but he could also tell when his line of work was too dangerous or frigid for a woman who looked like that.

"Good afternoon, Mr. Jonah. I'm Wanda. Allow me to take your jacket, and please follow me," she said as she held her arm out to him, her eyes fixed on his face. She knew how to maintain demanding eye contact. She guided Jonah into a room that seemed like a lavish version of a holding cell. There was a barred iron lock on the door but only on the outside. However, the inside of the room had a single sterile-looking bed, a gorgeous painting of the New York City skyline, and a massive window on the other end of the room. The window seemed to have a thin red line going around it, indicating that it had sensors.

A gown was placed on the foot of the bed. A soft mint green shift-like gown that resembled those that patients are placed in before surgery. *"Please wear this gown, Mr. Jonah,"* Wanda instructed as she gestured at the gown on the bed. *"You will be taken into our procedure room in a short while."*

"Wait ... what? What for? I didn't ask for anything," Jonah said, confused about everything. He was confused from the

moment he put that blindfold on, but since he was smart enough not to question Najib unnecessarily, he played along. As soon as he was taken into this strange place, a slight tinge of worry started to form in his core. And now this "procedure." The current happenings did not sit well with Jonah.

"Now, don't worry, Mr. Jonah. We need to remove the chip that has been placed in your shoulder," Wanda advised as soon as she saw the look of worry on Jonah's face.

Jonah knew he would be tracked, and if so, the location of this facility would be compromised. So, judging by the intensity of the security, he realized that the anonymity and privacy of these people were certainly crucial. They did not want to leave any single ground uncovered. After giving a relatively short amount of the necessary instructions, Wanda left the room, allowing Jonah to settle his mind into what was happening and what was about to happen. He paced the room, trying to wrap his mind around all he had just witnessed.

The apparent state-of-the-art look of the interior, the number of scientists roaming from one room to the next, and the facility's sheer size were a blunt show of wealth. He knew Prince Najib was a wealthy individual, but he did not know to what extent. But it was safe to say that this entire establishment was not just the work of one Prince Najib. He must have his hands dipped into plenty of other pies. Jonah wondered if there were other people involved in the work being done here. What that work was, though, was still a mystery to Jonah.

However, he knew for sure that he would soon be rid of the chip installed in his shoulder. Before leaving, Wanda had informed Jonah that they would have to drug him as it may have been too painful to pull out the chip from under his skin. Soon enough, Jonah was interrupted from his reverie while he was trying to figure everything out when Wanda arrived in the room, tailed by two of her assistants. They brought in a wheelchair and a tray containing substances to drug him to prepare for the procedure.

Wanda injected Jonah's left arm with a fluid-filled syringe, presumably a tranquilizer, to knock him out cold. *"It will be over before you know it, Mr. Jonah,"* Wanda said in a halfhearted attempt to calm his nerves about the situation.

"Just call me Jonah. I don't like that, Mr. shit," Jonah replied as he started feeling the effects of the tranquilizer already. His words started to slur. Both of Wanda's assistants took hold of Jonah and transferred him to the wheelchair. He was then wheeled to the procedure room as Wanda followed close behind. A red light turned on outside the door just as Jonah lost consciousness.

Chapter 7: Enemies

The procedure was short, with Wanda skillfully removing the chip from Jonah's shoulder. Jonah was then transferred to a different room after it was done. As the anesthesia from the tranquilizer wore off, Jonah slowly woke up and found himself in a fully furnished bedroom. His eyes scanned the room, unsure of where he was, when he suddenly remembered that he was in a facility in the middle of nowhere. The condition of the room and the location of the facility it was in further added to Jonah's surprise and confusion.

"Well, I'm alive, so I guess they did what needed to be done. Either way, I can't complain. The chip would've done more harm than good," Jonah said to himself.

Jonah then tried and got up from the bed and paced around the room to look at the furnishings. The room was intricately decorated and portrayed a rather fancy approach which meant it was clearly made that way to give the impression that he was supposed to relax in there. Jonah had been in the industry for far too long and knew that there was never a chance to take it easy in an unknown place, no matter what. Even if a friend somewhat owned it, if he could call Najib that.

After what seemed like an hour of rest in the lavishly decorated room, Wanda came in— this time in formal wear— and greeted Jonah. *"Hello, Jonah. I see you're recovering quite nicely,"* Wanda said. *"Did you get a chance to see the suit I got for you? It's right here,"* she gestured to the hand-carved wooden armoire on the other side of the bed. She opened one door and took out a crisp navy suit perfectly hung inside.

"Please change into this. We're waiting for you in the dining room," Wanda said as she handed the suit to Jonah and then glided out of the room. Every time she entered or left the room, Jonah couldn't help but stare at her well-toned legs. She did carry heels extraordinarily well.

Jonah took a good look at the suit hanger in his hand and admired it as soon as he saw the craftsmanship. It was Tom Ford, of course, because the tag sewn into the collar gave it away. Whoever Najib's partner was apparently had equal amounts of big bucks - judging by the amount they had spent on every single aspect of that facility and everything else they had splurged on. From the clean interior to the intricately decorated rooms and the thoroughly professional scientific individuals, no expense had been spared.

Jonah put on the suit and got ready. After one last look in the mirror, he left the room. As he made his way to the dining room adjacent to the guest room he was staying in, he observed everything he could lay his eyes on.

At the dinner table, Jonah was greeted by an enormous spread of food, far too much for just three people. Jonah sat at one end of the table, and Wanda sat in one of the neighboring chairs. There was another man who sat at the far end of the table. A stoic figure who looked like he was simply there to make sure Jonah did not try anything clever. He did not utter a sound and carefully listened to every word spoken at the table.

The man proceeded to put a recording device on the table to record the entire conversation, so the machine would catch anything he missed. The whole situation was a little bit uneasy and unusual compared to anything that had previously transpired in Jonah's experience in this line of work. But he went along with it, keeping his eyes and ears open.

"Relax, you're not in any danger anymore," Wanda spoke softly to Jonah, attempting to put him at ease. Not too comforted by her words, Jonah focused his attention on the lavish dinner in front of him. The meal looked like it was exquisitely planned and made to look its most delectable shade of enticing for Jonah.

There were no questions or answers exchanged at the dining table. That was an indication for Jonah that what he saw and experienced was all that it was. There would be no curious questions or explanations for any part of Jonah's visit. Simply put, he was taken to a safe facility to get his tracking chip taken out. That happened, and then he was offered lavish clothing and a meal to recover from the surgery-like procedure comfortably.

Jonah understood perfectly well that he was not on his turf, and that meant acting clever in any way might put him in danger. After the meal was done, Jonah was instructed to head to the exit, as there was a helicopter waiting for him on the helipad outside.

The pain in Jonah's shoulder was uncomfortable, but it was tolerable. As he made his way to the helicopter waiting to take him out of the facility, he had a feeling it would take him to the Prince. The silver lining was that the anesthetic had almost worn off, but his pace was still slowed, and he couldn't physically keep up with what was happening around him.

However, Jonah's mind was utterly active, and he attempted to understand everything the people around him were doing. The pain from the chip removal procedure made Jonah's arm numb, but he had been in more challenging situations before. He knew how to act as if nothing bothered him. He knew how to fake it till it reached an uncompromising space.

The helicopter ride did not take too long as it reached another remote airplane runway. This time, the runway was a private one that reserved aircraft for celebrities and such.

As the helicopter was about to land, Jonah looked out the window and noticed a familiar face. Prince Najib was waiting patiently near the airplane hangar beside a fancy private plane. There was a smile on Najib's face as he saw the helicopter land. Jonah got off the helicopter and walked to Najib. A million questions ran through his mind as he was filled with confusion. He wanted to ask about the entire experience he had just had.

As soon as Najib faced Jonah, he went in for a tight embrace, followed by a kiss on both cheeks. Of course, Jonah was not fond of it, but this was what his friend did every time they both came into contact in person. It was the Prince's way of letting Jonah know that the environment would be friendly and that he had nothing to fear. But as long as Jonah had been in this line of work, there was never a time when he could not keep his mind on alert. So, it wasn't even a matter of fight or flight; it was his default mechanism.

Following the greeting, Prince Najib led Jonah into the private plane and made it clear that he wanted to discuss something vital. Once inside, the doors were locked, and the pilot prepared for take-off. The Prince sat next to Jonah and said, *"Now that we're here and safe, I presume you have questions for me, Jonah."*

Jonah took a moment to register his friend's question, all the while looking out the window as the plane started to take off. Then, finally, he looked at Najib and simply said with a smirk, *"Well, shit, what gave you that idea?"*

Instantly, Najib laughed, and so did Jonah. After that, both men relaxed, and there were no signs of hostility inside that private jet. Then, after a hearty laugh, Najib turned to Jonah and said, *"Jokes apart, my friend, I think it is time that I told you about the facility you were taken to get your chip removed. But I must say, all I can tell you is that it is a place of safety. A place where I can go and know that I am completely in control of my surroundings. Everything else.... You will know when the time comes."*

As Jonah had suspected, the Prince was not going to let the true purpose of that facility be revealed. However, there might come a time when such a thing could be possible.

"But Jonah, my friend, there is a matter of grave importance that I want to discuss with you." Najib continued, *"The attack on us earlier was one of many."*

"What do you mean, Najib?" Jonah asked, attempting to connect the dots within his mind.

"For the past year, the man who attacked us with his goons has been targeting us without delay." Najib seemingly measured his answer and continued, *"I have noticed that he has a pattern. He attacks when I am about to meet with a friend or an alliance. This time, he caught wind that you and I were going to meet in person, and he struck again. I am afraid that all my friends and I are in danger because he has set his sights on my destruction."*

Jonah was in shock. He tried his best to maintain an air of calm, but he was failing because his face could not lie at the thought of his dear friend being in grave danger. Finally, after a brief inhale and exhale, he said to Najib, *"Why didn't you tell me anything earlier? I could have helped you. You know that."*

"I understand, my friend," Najib replied. *"But please see it from my point of view. I thought that I was protecting you by maintaining my distance."*

"Najib, I can protect myself," Jonah rebutted. *"I am surprised that you never shared this information that your life has been in danger for quite some time now."*

Najib could sense the disappointment in Jonah's voice and on his face because, at that moment, he sighed and then replied, *"I know that now."*

"Good, now tell me the entire story," Jonah inquired. *"tell me. Why is this man targeting you, and do you know what he plans to do next?"*

Before Najib could even continue, Jonah was already thinking of ways he could help his dear friend in this battle against an unknown enemy.

Chapter 8: Suspicious

Jonah waited patiently for his friend to answer the burning question of who was targeting him and why.

"My friend, I do not know why exactly he is targeting me, except for the obvious reason, which could be money," Najib replied. *"Other than that, your guess is as good as mine. What I do know is that there must be a much bigger reason for that man's punishment-worthy actions. But I have no way of finding out what they are."*

"Tell me, who has he targeted so far?" Jonah asked.

"Oh, I am sure about that part," Najib replied. *"He has been targeting my nearest and dearest. But not only that, he has information on my allies and who they are because he has been targeting them as well."*

"That is frightening," Jonah said with a sigh. *"To constantly fear an attack on anyone you hold dear. That is a feeling I would not wish upon anyone. Let alone you, my friend."*

"Jonah, he took aim at my childhood friends and the woman I love!" Najib exclaimed.

"Who? The Peruvian woman you introduced me to once?" Jonah questioned. *"You're in love with her?"*

"Yes, and once she was attacked, the fear truly set in," Najib replied. The solemn feeling in his voice was heartbreaking. This was one of the most powerful men Jonah ever knew. In fact, Najib, the Prince, was *the* most powerful figure he knew. So, to see him look fearful was instead a humbling sensation for Jonah. He had never seen the Prince appear so in search of answers and contention as in that moment inside that private jet. Empathy was not Jonah's strong suit, he knew that, but at that moment, he wanted to help his friend in any way he could.

"I know one thing for sure, Jonah," the Prince sighed heavily and said. *"The show must go on. I cannot act as if all this is not slowing me down. I have things I wish to accomplish. So, all this must take the passenger seat. I shall have to look at everything simultaneously because facing one thing and not the other is not something I can bring myself to do."*

"I can understand that, but how can I help?" Jonah asked.

"I had arranged for us to meet that day when the attack happened because I wanted your help with orchestrating an auction," Najib proclaimed. *"I know now that because I arranged that meeting, I put your life in danger and that you could have died due to that. Although I can acknowledge this truth, I also know that at this moment, you are the only person I trust with this information, Jonah."*

The Prince took a deep breath and sighed. He clearly looked like he had the weight of the world on his shoulders.

Jonah could not imagine being in a similar position. He thought to himself that the Prince's entire persona was not one that came without its challenges and complications. The challenges of having not only your own life be under threat but having your dear ones and your connections targeted specifically and so openly was a whole other ball game.

However, Jonah was well aware that the Prince was capable of handling dangers to his own life, as this was the entire reason he was so comfortable with the challenges within this life of uncertainty. He knew that the Prince survived and thrived within this line of work, but at that moment, as he told his story to Jonah, he appeared as if things had gone way above what he had predicted. But still, Jonah had to look at the Prince and give him props that he was handling it all much better than Jonah would have if he were in similar circumstances.

"I have to say that the reason I came to you, Jonah, was because I wanted you to understand the sensitivity of this auction," Najib continued. *"Although my current state of events has slowed it down a little, the auction has been planned for quite a while now. And although I have conducted and arranged many such events in my time, this one will certainly be the most elaborate and important."*

Jonah was well aware of how vital the auctions were for Prince Najib, and he was pretty famous for them as well. The main reason for that was the obvious one which meant the Prince was not just in his name. He was true royalty from the Middle East. Although Jonah did not know the full extent of his riches, he had a distinct inclination. The auctions the Prince usually was known for and arranged were nothing less than the finest exhibitions of opulence. These auctions contained delicate pieces of art, and artifacts gathered from all over the world and curated especially by the Prince himself.

As a result, the auctions had gained notoriety and the attention of people with some pretty heavy pockets around the world. In addition, the auctions had become a ground for people from different areas and professions globally. The people who were scheduled to attend were regulars and newcomers alike, coming from clean and criminal backgrounds. The auction had become a playground for all of them to mingle and catch up.

Jonah could sense that there was no way the Prince's current state of affairs and his challenges would hinder the upcoming auction. So canceling the auction or even delaying it was not going to be an option. People were going to fly in from all over the world, and the artifacts had already been curated. The Prince was not going to let the ill intentions of one enemy get the better of him, so he wanted Jonah to help him out. He was confident that the only person he could trust was Jonah because he was well aware of how sensitive the entire procedure for the Prince's auctions was.

Furthermore, since the Prince had been in this dangerous line of work for longer than Jonah, he knew the importance of keeping up appearances. So, if he even considered canceling the auction, the attendees would get wind of something amiss. Since they were high officials, they had methods of obtaining information about events and people that sparked their curiosity. The Prince canceling one of his famous auctions would be nothing less than that. So, all in all, Najib required Jonah's expertise to make sure everything from the plane ride onward would go as smoothly as possible.

The goal was the auction's proceeding and the secrecy of the Prince's attacks, and Jonah was going to be the perfect candidate for that. On top of that, Jonah was Najib's friend, so he could not just say no.

"I understand why you need my help, Najib, and you shall have it," Jonah told the Prince. *"Without any second thought. You are my friend, and this is a no-brainer. I assure you that we will take down your enemy together."*

Once the Prince heard those words from Jonah, it seemed like the weight on his shoulders was slightly lifted. He appeared to relax somewhat, and as he did, he embraced Jonah once again. *"My friend, you cannot begin to imagine how grateful I am to have you by my side,"* Najib said.

As the conversation between Najib and Jonah came to an end, the private jet they were in was coming to a landing stop. After processing all that the Prince had to say, Jonah's instincts had already started sending out subtle alert signals. He knew that every time he received these signals, he would be vigilant and heed their warning. So, for now, he knew that he would keep his instincts active and only talk to the Prince when he got a moment with him in private. At that moment, they both got off the private jet and proceeded on their way to the Prince's home.

The entire ride to his home, the Prince assured Jonah that he would be welcome to stay for as long as he liked, especially because the Prince made it clear he wanted Jonah around. Something about having a familiar person on the premises to satisfy his reliance.

Jonah had his suspicion instincts on the entire time. He was certain that there would not be a single moment of ease for the Prince and that his dear friend would be on edge until he found the man responsible for these attacks.

Targeted attacks of physical harm would put anyone on edge, but if they are not just for you but your family and any person in your close personal circle as well, then your nerves are bound to be in knots every day—from the second you wake up in the morning to the moment you lay down to sleep. Every subtle spark of instinct inside Jonah's body told him that there had to be someone within the Prince's ranks acting as a spy.

According to Jonah's rising suspicions, someone who might know the inner dealings of the Prince's contacts and his associate circle might be using them to get to him and help destroy him. The way Prince Najib had disclosed the entire story to Jonah, he knew there had to be someone within his ranks to help the people behind all this. This was the only theory that came to Jonah's mind and made sense since he was well aware that Najib was an extremely private man.

Jonah knew for certain that Jim, one of the men that picked him up in the van near his home, would be aware of when the auction was happening. It all made sense; there had to be a spy, and they had to be working with Jim while they also stayed by the Prince's side. So, since Jonah knew how private his friend Najib liked to keep his life, this was the only logical explanation. This theory also meant that Jonah would have trouble getting the Prince alone, especially since the guards accompanied Najib everywhere, even to the toilets.

However, Jonah needed to think of a sure-fire way— and fast— if he wanted to have an honest conversation with just the Prince. So, Jonah decided to stick around with the Prince within a short distance so that he could catch the Prince when he was alone. Jonah did not know who to trust and who not to in that place. Even though the house belonged to his friend and he could roam around freely, he still wanted to keep to himself. He just needed a small window to reach the Prince by himself so that he could share this information at the right time.

Chapter 9: The Walls Have Ears/Hard to Reach

The Prince's house was massive, and there were plenty of rooms he could choose to be in, but the entire area was heavily guarded. Jonah noticed that every security team member seemed sterner and more hyper-aware than usual, presumably because the last attack on the Prince was not too long ago. So it was only fair to assume that they were not only instructed by Najib to watch every nook and cranny of his home but also to be aware of Jonah's safety since he was staying with him until the auction.

Jonah predicted that the entire security team was aware of the attacks on Najib and that all his friends were also being targeted. That is why whenever Jonah would leave his room to wander the corridors and look for Najib, he would find a guard stationed outside his door, lurking in the halls and near the other rooms. This level of security detail would be extremely difficult to maneuver and reach Najib in his privacy. So Jonah decided to keep an eye out for a window of opportunity and case the place for clues.

For now, he went straight to his room. He needed to think about how he was going to navigate the next few hours. Catering to his intuition, Jonah was certain that at least one person within the Prince's entourage or security detail was acting as a snitch, so he wanted to cover as much ground as he could to get a sense of who it could be. Either way, Jonah knew he could not give anyone any indication he was up to something or that he suspected the staff.

So, he scribbled a note on a small piece of paper to give to Najib during a casual handshake when they would meet at dinner.

"We need to talk. Urgent!" He wrote on the note. But as he contemplated his actions in the future, Jonah heard a knock on his bedroom door. The Prince's butler, who seemed to be European, was there to let him know that dinner would be served in five minutes and that he was expected to show up in the dining room.

"Will the Prince be there?" Jonah asked the butler.

"Of course, sir," the butler replied. *"I make sure that he does not miss a meal. Especially under the current circumstances."*

"I am glad," Jonah faintly smiled and said. *"I shall be there in the dining room in two minutes."*

As that small conversation ended, Jonah closed the door and prepared himself to try and alert his friend during dinner. He knew he did not have any proof just yet, so he decided that it would be best to simply give Prince Najib an indication of signs of disloyalty within his ranks. Jonah needed to let Najib know why he had these intuitions and that he wanted to keep his dear friend safe.

After a couple of minutes passed and Jonah decided how to move forward, he left his room and made his way to the dining room. Upon arrival, Jonah could see that Najib was already sitting in his chair, about to drink a glass of water. Jonah sat down in the chair that the butler pulled out for him.

"Najib, I was wondering if I could speak to you privately," Jonah said as he unfolded his napkin onto his lap. *"I know guards are meant to stay around you at all times, but my friend, this information could help you greatly."*

"Hmm... You can tell me now, Jonah. These are my most trusted men," Najib replied. *"They know everything about my life. I assure you."*

"I am sure they are, my friend," Jonah rebutted politely. *"But as your dear companion, I hope to get just a few moments with you to have a heart-to-heart conversation. You can allow me that surely, can you not?"*

There was a strange look of dismay on Najib's face. It was as if he wanted to tell Jonah something, but he just could not bring himself to say something. It was as if something was stopping him from saying what he wanted to say. Now, Jonah was perceptive, sometimes a little too much for his own good. But this time, he knew something was troubling the Prince, so he diverted the conversation accordingly. He knew he had to find another moment to talk to Najib in detail.

"On second thought...." Jonah continued. *"You know what? Let us just enjoy the food for now, and we can talk over a drink some other time."*

"Yes, I would like that very much, my friend," Najib replied solemnly.

Just as Najib finished his reply, he and Jonah were interrupted by one of his men. He came up to Najib and whispered something in his ear. As much as Jonah tried, he could not hear a word of what his friend was being told.

"Is it necessary to go now? Can't I just be done with a peaceful meal with my friend and then handle every task I am supposed to?" the Prince asked his subordinate.

"Sorry, sir," the guard answered firmly. *"But the matter is urgent and needs to be handled at this very moment."*

"Very well," the Prince said curtly and rose from his chair, as did Jonah. This was his moment to shake his hand and pass the note to Najib. Najib swiftly got hold of the note and put it into his jacket pocket.

"I apologize, Jonah, but you will have to excuse me. I must go and handle some business reluctantly. I hope we can have that drink soon and catch up with everything then. Please enjoy the dinner," Najib said as he made his way to the exit door. But before he left, he directed his attention to his butler and said, *"Please see to it that Mr. Jonah is well taken care of and that all food is to his liking."*

"Do you want me to come with you, Najib?" Jonah asked as he stood at a distance.

"Oh no, that will not be necessary, my friend," Najib answered. *"It is just a small errand, and I will be back before you know it."*

For a moment, Najib considered the worried expression on Jonah's face, and since he could not reveal the fact that he was worried as well, he said, *"I know that it might sound like a cliché, my friend, but do not worry. Just trust me. I shall be back soon."* Then, before Jonah could bring himself to stop Najib, he was whisked away by his guards and left.

Jonah decided it would be best to carry on this air of casual behavior since he did not want any member of the Prince's staff to even consider that he suspected something was wrong. Jonah merely wanted everyone in that house to believe that he was just staying with the Prince because he was worried his friend's life was in danger. Therefore, he played the part of a subdued guest and tried not to arouse any suspicion.

Soon, while contemplating what he would do next, Jonah finished his dinner, thanked the butler for the meal, and left the dining room. But as he made his way to the bedroom, he could sense someone following him all the way to the room.

Jonah was a well-versed individual in this game of cat and mouse, so he knew exactly how to navigate an air of intrigue. He walked as casually as possible, and when he reached his bedroom door, he opened the handle with one hand and turned around to look behind him. It was the butler.

He paused midway and said, "*Forgive me for following you, sir. I was merely coming after you to let you know that I was told by your friend, the Prince, that kindly do not roam around on the premises on your own. It will not be safe.*"

"*I understand,*" Jonah replied politely to the butler. "*I shall stay in my room.*"

"*Very well, Mr. Jonah,*" the butler said as he turned to leave.

"*Oh wait.... I'm sorry, but I was just wondering if you could tell me your name,*" Jonah called out to the butler as he was leaving. "*I have a phone in my room, and if I need something, I shall ask for you.*"

The butler smiled and replied, "*My name is Tobias, sir. You can ask for Tobias from the phone in your room if you require something.*"

"*Alright... Thank you, Tobias,*" Jonah continued. "*And please give my compliments to the chef. The dinner was exquisite.*"

"Will do, sir," Tobias said as he turned on his heel and swiftly left.

Jonah closed his door and locked it from the inside. He knew that a simple single lock would not protect him much, and he proceeded to check his jacket pocket that was hung on an armoire in the corner of the room. Jonah had been an expert in this game of secrets and intrigue for way too long.

He always had a small revolver and a dagger hidden in the lining of his jacket pocket. He took off the jacket from the hanger and laid it flat beneath his pillow, then laid down on the bed. With all the mysterious vibes he saw and felt that day, he decided that the best thing to do would be to wait until Najib returned to the house and plan the next move.

Chapter 10: Dark Secrets

After the many years that Jonah had spent in this industry known as a glorified cat-and-mouse chase by the people who worked within it, his intuitions and instincts had been sharpened to the very best of his abilities. He was always aware of the people near him and how they would move. His senses had heightened over the years, making him a considerably light sleeper.

As Jonah was asleep in one of the guest rooms in Najib's home, his senses were on high alert, and he woke up instantly when he heard someone trying to sneak into the room. Without moving much of his body, he snuck his hand under his pillow and grabbed the revolver.

Jonah subtly moved his other hand to the lamp switch on the bedside table. Then, in one fell swoop, he instantly switched on the light, turned, and sat on the bed while pointing the gun directly at the intruder.

"Woah, woah, woah... It's only me!" Najib repeatedly said in a hurry, raising his arms in the air. His voice was low as a whisper as he came near Jonah.

"Jesus Christ, man! Why are you sneaking in? This is your own place!" Jonah said as he put down the gun.

Najib put a hand to Jonah's lips, pointedly looked over to the light, and whispered to Jonah, "*Cut the light. No one outside must know that I am in here.*"

Completely confused, Jonah did exactly as his friend said. "*Now, would you mind explaining why you felt the need to sneak in?*" He asked Najib.

"*Patience, my friend, I will tell you,*" Najib replied as he proceeded to sit down on the side of Jonah's bed. "*I read your note, and come to think of it, I know exactly what you want to talk to me about.*"

"*How?*" Jonah asked, perplexed. "*How do you know? We barely got to talk ever since we came here.*"

"*My friend, I have known you long and well enough to understand when you are facing a predicament,*" Najib replied calmly. "*But yes, I do have something important to discuss with you. Something that simply could not wait till morning because I do not know what could happen. These days, I just never know when my life could take a drastic turn.*"

Jonah simply sighed in response and then instinctually looked toward the window. He then replied, "*Najib, to tell you the truth, I have had my suspicions for quite a while now. I am aware that you have a trusted circle around you and that most of the people here have been with you for a long time. But I must compel you to reconsider.*"

Najib sat up straight and paid close attention to every word Jonah said. His expression looked like he was internally agreeing with what his friend was suggesting.

"Ever since we both were attacked on that tarmac; my instincts have been on high alert. Of course, I did not want to scare you, well, even more than you already may be," Jonah continued, *"but I have been keeping a close eye on the members of your security detail. Now, I understand that you must trust them with your life, considering the level of privacy you like to keep in your life. But do you think that there could be a slight chance that even one of them could be a spy?"*

After carefully listening to what Jonah had to say, Najib sighed before responding, *"I must admit, I do not believe there is just one. I say this because I have been suspecting my team of treachery and deceit for some time now. Not all of them, perhaps, but I am sure of the fact that there are at least a couple of rats in the mix."*

Just then, Najib got up from where he was sitting and walked across the room. He looked like his body was having trouble digesting too many realities at once. He not only faced the danger of losing the people he held dear but was also aware of the fact that the very people who were responsible for guarding his life were a danger to him too. These were the people he had looked after for many years. He had given them a home under his roof and even taken care of their families.

Jonah could clearly see that this information was rattling Najib from within. He was aware that the first and foremost thing that formed a friendship between himself and Najib was loyalty and the value attached to it. It was the closest belief to both their hearts as they thought that they would perish without it in the lives they led. Therefore, it was vital to have a deep sense of loyalty among their ranks, so they could have one less thing to worry about in their jobs and during their missions.

After taking a couple of slow and measured paces around Jonah's room, Najib stood still while resting both his hands on the windowsill. Finally, Jonah got up from his bed, came over to Najib, and placed a hand on his friend's shoulder.

Najib's head sank, and he sighed deeply. He knew that if he and his trusted friend Jonah were having the same suspicions, they were most likely to be true.

"Do you know how much I have done for these fools?" Najib solemnly said as he looked outside at the courtyard view.

Jonah stood silent and let his friend continue. He knew that this revelation, or better yet, the confirmation of both their suspicions, was quite similar to heartbreak for Najib.

Then, after a brief spell of silence, Jonah asked, *"Najib, tell me something. By chance, were you aware that you would face an attack that day on the tarmac?"*

Since Najib had confessed that he had been suspicious of treachery and insubordination among his security, it could have been a valid possibility that he knew the attack was coming. So, upon this question from Jonah, Najib looked over at him, and Jonah knew. His suspicions were correct all along.

Najib bowed his head again and, without moving from his place, said, *"Forgive me, Jonah. I knew an attack was coming the day we were scheduled to meet on that tarmac. By that time, life-threatening and vicious attacks had only happened to members of my family and my connections who were considerably well-known."*

Jonah simply took a few paces backward. But Najib continued, *"No one knew about the friendship I shared with you. I wanted to find out if the man behind all this was aware of our connection. So, I had no other way to confirm my suspicions. Please do not be angry with me because Jonah, I knew you could handle yourself, and I was right there with you."*

Jonah folded his arms, took a deep breath, and responded, *"Najib... I am not angry with you. Of course, I understand that you needed to confirm your suspicions and why it was crucial for you to do so. I just feel like you could have told me about this beforehand so that at least I could have been more prepared."*

"I know, my friend, trust me. I know." Najib turned from the window and said, *"But please understand that I simply could not risk it. You know how closely I am being watched by*

my security—they are aware of mostly all communication I do. So, there was no way for me to make you aware."

Najib took a seat on the armchair across the room and continued, *"Also, if anyone could even sense that you were aware before you and I met, then I don't know what could happen to you. At least when we were by each other's side, we could protect each other and make sure that we both got out of there alive."*

Jonah knew that his friend was right to act the way he did and that he was being genuine. Things could have gone way more downhill if the opposing side had caught wind of what he and Najib were planning.

"I can sense that you are disappointed in me, Jonah. But please, try and see it from my point of view," Najib said. *"I am sure you will be able to see my predicament. So, tell me, can I trust you to stand beside me? And can I trust you with my life?"*

Just then, Jonah went and sat on the armchair beside the one Najib had been sitting on.

"Everything that has happened... and everything that will happen... none of it will make me any less of a friend to you, Najib," Jonah said solemnly. *"So, not to get emotional or anything, but it seems that I have to. We are still brothers in arms or just brothers in general. I can understand why you made your decisions. I just wish I could have taken some of your misery and done more for you. I swear that you have my word. I will protect you with my life."*

Najib let out a small laugh as relief washed over his face and said, *"You are right, once again. Has there ever been a time when you were wrong?"*

"Once or twice—give or take," Jonah replied, chuckling.

That was the moment Jonah and Najib realized they were like brothers, even more than their own kin. There was a level of understanding between the two that established that neither of them would put the other's life in danger on purpose. Even though they knew they could encounter missions separately, Jonah would always miss being in Najib's company, and the same would be true for Najib.

"Let us just make a pact tonight, my friend, and shake on it," Najib said while holding out his hand.

"What's that?" replied Jonah as he grabbed his friend's hand.

"To never let any suspicion come in between each other and that we will always have each other's back." Najib continued, *"No matter where we are or what we are working on, we are brothers."*

Jonah smiled, firmly shook Najib's hand, and said, *"Deal!"*

Chapter 11: The Auction

After the intense conversation Jonah had with Najib, he went back to sound sleep as his friend left the room. Now that Jonah knew Najib was aware of mutiny within his staff, he at least had one less detail to worry about. The fact that his dear friend not only agreed with his suspicions but also carried them from the start meant that they would truly be by each other's side from here on out.

Jonah was woken up the next morning by a knock on his bedroom door. As he woke, he asked, *"Yes? Who is it?"*

"Sir, this is Tobias," Najib's butler answered from the other side of the door. Upon hearing this, Jonah got up from his bed and instantly went to the door to open it and answer.

"Yes, Tobias, I am awake now," Jonah said as he opened the door. *"I was just about to change."*

"Yes, quite right, sir," Tobias said. *"Breakfast is almost ready, and there is a car waiting outside to take you and Master Najib to the auction venue when you are done. This is why I would suggest that you get ready for that now."*

"Oh. You're right. I will do that. Thank you, Tobias," Jonah replied. *"I will be in the dining room in just a few minutes."*

Tobias tilted and bowed his head slightly and then turned around to leave. Jonah closed the door, locked it, and quickly freshened up. As he put on his suit, he made sure to strap his handy and easily concealable gun to the waistband and under his suit jacket. He was definitely not about to take any chances that day by only taking one of his weapons. So, after his gun, he strapped a dagger on the side of one ankle as he wore his leather penny loafers.

Jonah was aware that his day was going to be on high alert throughout, at least until he and Najib returned safely home after the auction. So, after getting ready, mentally, and weapon-wise, he went to the breakfast table and saw that Najib had also just arrived. They both pulled out their chairs in unison and gave each other a knowing smile.

"Good morning, Najib," Jonah said to him.

"Good morning to you as well, my friend," Najib replied. *"I do hope it stays that way."*

"Yes, you and me both," Jonah said as he sat down and pulled his napkin onto his lap. *"How are you feeling about today?"*

Najib contemplated how to answer for a minute as he poured a tall glass of water. *"I am alright, considering the circumstances. As long as we are together, I am sure all will be fine,"* Najib said as he raised his glass to Jonah.

"I agree," Jonah smiled. The two friends continued with their breakfast, and after finishing their tea, they both got up from the table and made their way outside onto the

driveway. A car was waiting in the middle, surrounded by two security-detailed cars on either end, Abdul standing next to one, waiting for them to join. All of Najib's security was made to prepare for the auction, as it was the most anticipated event for the Prince.

Everyone around Najib was aware of the growing threat to the Prince's life, and so everyone, including Jonah, was ready in case things ended up going south. They were ready for anything as soon as they all got into their respective cars. Initially, Jonah's job was to be an auctioneer that day, but the job description did not cover protecting friends whose lives were threatened by powerful enemies.

Therefore, Jonah took it upon himself to not only look out for potential threats to Najib's life but also for any suspicious behavior on the security's part. Soon enough, they reached the venue for the auction. The first thing Jonah noticed was that the people in attendance looked even more dangerous this time around.

Moreover, the location for the venue was an undisclosed one, and only those who had received an invite from the Prince himself were told when and where to attend. Everything about the details of the auction was given on a need-to-know basis, where only the coordinates of the location were disclosed.

This method was fool proof only because it would allow the Prince to narrow down who could be involved in the attacks being conducted so maliciously on him and his close friends and family. In addition, Najib gave a copy of the list of attendees to Jonah on the way to the venue and told him in great detail about the folks he mainly had his suspicions for.

Even though Jonah was aware that the Prince was known for having successful auctions, by the looks of it all, it seemed as if it was ready to go to the dumps even before starting. The security detail took its place on all corners of the venue. They were posted on the outside and the inside, respectively, as they were given a briefing about how to handle any suspicious activity and to protect Najib at all costs.

Everyone around the Prince looked tense, but Jonah was in his most alert condition as soon as he reached the venue. He was ready just to be done with it and be out of the potential danger presented at this event. Jonah walked beside Najib, escorting him to his seating near the auction stage.

Najib's seat was behind bulletproof glass as it looked like a mini cabin. This looked highly unusual for most auctions, but then again, this was certainly not any ordinary auction. Along with many valuable items being offered at this event, the most important one was a rather high-end cultural artifact that belonged to one of Najib's Egyptian ancestors.

Jonah was unsure of exactly how old the artifact was, but he was certain that it was valuable enough that every single person in the audience had their eyes lit up as they saw it on the pedestal on stage. Everyone wanted to get their hands on the rare find, and they were willing to do anything to get it. This is because the audience included people who were used to getting their own way, and the Prince knew that.

Najib was notorious for hosting these and even more so for having the audience of these auctions come from all parts of the world. These auctions were where people from the seemingly good side of the business world collided with the bad ones. This was a place where the lines were completely blurred. What was good and what was bad was all about their perspectives. So when the time came for the most important piece of the event to be auctioned off, the paddles rose rather hesitantly in the audience.

Everyone was aware that there were people in attendance who were willing to shoot openly if they were not given what they had their eyes on the entire night. This is why Jonah not only stayed in close range of Najib's spot but also made sure that his eyes were on the audience and their movements. Najib maintained eye contact with Jonah and knew that as soon as he felt something was amiss, he would be instantly alerted.

Surprisingly, the auction went on without a hitch. When the time came for the artifact of the hour to be sold off, at that exact moment, Jonah saw one security guard at the far end of the entrance speak into his attached microphone. Then, he saw the guard instantly rush outside. This was Jonah's cue that the commotion was going to begin just as the auction was coming to an end.

As soon as one guard went outside to see what he was being called for, another guard from the other end of the hall signaled Jonah to stay close to the Prince. Jonah responded by moving from his position and going right by the Prince's side without arousing any semblance of suspicion from the crowd. But little did he know, things were about to get a lot louder outside. Nevertheless, Jonah ensured that he would fulfill his duties as the auctioneer, which meant he would stay by Najib's side and control the proceedings as well.

As the auctioneer, Jonah yelled, *"And the star of the show tonight has just been sold to the lucky gentleman in seat number 44. Congratulations, sir!"*

There was clapping happening left, right, and center as the piece had fortunately gone to the most dangerous and richest man in the room. He was a known don of the most powerful mafia family in New York. His family was feared as being the top dog in the mafia for the past eight generations. So even though Jonah was not quite sure why the artifact was so valuable, he was convinced of the fact that it was a good thing that it had gone to the most powerful man in attendance, as it meant that no one would dare to fight over it.

Meanwhile, as the audience was busy clapping, a loud explosion went off outside. It was followed by three more consecutive explosions, with only half a second between each of them. Jonah did not waste a moment after he heard them as he instantly covered Najib and pulled him straight behind his frame. It was fortunate that the Prince was behind bulletproof glass to begin with. Shrapnel from the blasts outside could not reach him.

However, the attendees panicked as they hurriedly ducked under the venue tables as shots rang out outside. Each of the attendees had apparently signaled their own security because men came in from the second entrance of the venue and took them all toward the individually parked vehicles on the other side of the building. At the same time, Jonah and Najib stuck together like glue as Jonah took out his gun and took Najib to hide behind the stage.

Najib had a look of utter fear on his face as he clutched his friend's arm. *"Najib, look at me! Look at me."* Jonah urged the Prince as he wanted to stop looking around everywhere just to see if the attacker would come in.

Upon Jonah's plea, Najib looked at him. *"I do not know who to trust, Jonah! And it is happening again,"* Najib blurted out as he was having slight trouble breathing from the smoke that flew inside the venue due to the blast.

"I will not let anything happen to you!" Jonah said to him as he attempted to stop Najib from panicking. *"Just stay with me. I know you want to get to the man who is doing this, but you have to get to safety first."*

Chapter 12: Run

The bullets rang out like fireworks outside the venue, and it felt like it had been going on forever, consuming multiple members of Najib's security detail in the process. The crowd seated for the auction looked like it was erupting into chaos in slow motion. None of the mafiosos or dignitaries could have predicted they would need to use their security guards at a simple auction. But, as it turned out, they would not only be making use of those guards but actually losing them in the fight outside in the courtyard.

The only thing on Jonah's mind was his dear friend's safety and that he needed to get him to a space where he could be out of reach of the spraying bullets. There was a chance that the perpetrators could enter the venue at any given moment after they got done with the guards outside. Moreover, from the sounds of it, it was not going to take much longer for them to figure out where Najib had gone off to if Jonah did not think fast. So, he looked for the best possible solution to getting Najib out of there.

Jonah then thought of an idea that would not only get him and Najib out of there as fast as possible but also buy them some time until the events outside subsided. He knew that the adversary must have taken hold of the venue from all angles outside and would notice instantly if Najib showed his face.

"Najib.... Do you trust me?" Jonah asked the Prince as he escorted him to the back of the auction stage door.

"Huh?" Najib answered, a little dazed from listening to the constant gunshots outside. *"What do you mean? Of course, I do."*

"Good, because I have an idea, and I have a feeling that you're not going to like it." Jonah continued in a whispered tone, *"But please, trust me, my friend."*

Najib nodded in agreement, and that was Jonah's cue to let Abdul know what he was thinking. While Abdul was guarding the door from the inside and keeping a lookout as to when the enemies would enter the venue, Jonah tapped him on the shoulder. *"Abdul, I want you to listen to me and listen closely. As soon as you see the men enter the venue, distract them."*

"What do you want me to do for that, Jonah?" Abdul asked sincerely.

"Shoot as many as you can, flip a couple of tables and chairs, and then instantly get out of there," Jonah replied. *"We want you alive. So, while you are doing that, I will take Najib outside because the men will be diverting their attention inside. No one would be watching the back entrance, and that will give Najib and me some room to make our way to the getaway car parked nearby."*

Just as Jonah finished, Najib spoke, *"Wait, I think we can make this plan a little better."* Just then, he took off his hat, his scarf, and the long bulky chain he was wearing around his neck and handed it all to Abdul. *"Wear these and take off your jacket."* Najib gestured to the black jacket Abdul had on that was similar to the ones worn by all members of his security detail. By that time, Abdul had figured out what was about to happen. He was about to join the ongoing fight outside, subtly dressed as the Prince.

He took the items Najib had handed over and put them on exactly how Najib would wear them. *"Do not worry, sir, I can handle myself,"* Abdul said as he saw the hesitant expression on Najib's face. *"I will meet you on the other side."*

Just as Abdul finished his sentence, the three men heard gunshots from the other side of the door, and they all gave each other one last reassuring look. *"Oh, and I almost forgot, leave the premises as soon as you two get to the car,"* Abdul said as he got up to adjust his hat one more time. *"Sir, you know where to go."* He said these words while looking directly at the Prince and went out.

Abdul sneakily made his way to the other side of the hall, and since the men had just entered the space strapped with firearms, they figured the man they were seeing at the far end of the hall was the Prince trying to escape. One of the men shouted at Abdul and said, *"You! Stop moving!"* Now, this was his cue to divert the men who entered to the other side of the venue and away from the direction of the stage door. That was the plan. Abdul was going to divert the remaining men from the gunfight to the other side of the venue and lock them into an isolated room. This would bide the Prince and Jonah some time to escape.

Meanwhile, Jonah and Najib had been sneakily looking through a peephole in the door. So, as soon as they saw the men running off after Abdul, Jonah and Najib made their way out of the back door of the venue. The two made sure they were running as fast as possible and without making any loud sounds because if, by chance, there were any men outside still on the lookout for the Prince, Jonah would not be able to do much on his own. No matter how skilled he was.

Jonah and Najib could still hear the gunshots going off inside the venue, but there were some left on the other side of the auction venue, near the entrance. Those were Najib's remaining security, trying to fend off as many enemies as they could. Both men ran toward the getaway car and instantly took their places inside, with Jonah in the driver's seat and Najib in the passenger seat beside him. Jonah could feel the adrenaline still pumping through him as he adjusted the steering wheel and put the car into gear.

"Hang tight, my friend, and put your seat belt on," Jonah instructed Najib. *"I don't want you flying out of the car after we have barely escaped from the fireworks back there."*

Najib looked at Jonah perplexed, knowing it was a joke, and said, *"Uh, yeah, sure. Just drive, my friend."*

As Jonah steered the car out of the driveway, they both could still hear the gunshots going off in the background. They knew for sure that whoever had attacked this time knew the Prince would be there and had come fully prepared. They had apparently been aware of the fact that the Prince did not miss one of his yearly auctions and would surely show up at the venue. The lengths that the adversary had gone through this time were much more elaborate and extensive.

The enemies were more in number, but they were still, thankfully, dumb enough to follow a figure who merely resembled the Prince's silhouette. Therefore, Najib and Jonah were able to get away from the commotion without really being harmed.

After Jonah had successfully gotten the car out of the premises, Najib sighed loudly and put his head back in his seat. He then said, *"Please tell me that Abdul and Omar will make it out of there alive and join us later?"*

Omar was second-in-command to Abdul in Najib's security team.

"I'm sure you will see them soon," Jonah sighed and replied. *"They are skilled enough to handle anything, so you don't have to worry about them like that."*

Najib heard Jonah's words, visibly relaxed, and said, *"You're right. They are the best that I have, so why do I need to worry?"*

"Exactly," Jonah replied. *"Now tell me the direction where I need to go because we are about to arrive at an intersection, and then the city ends."*

"Just take this highway straight to the edge of the city until you see the starting points of the desert," Najib added. *"Reach that point, and I will tell you the rest later."*

"Okay, if you say so," Jonah replied, as he knew his friend would tell him where exactly they were heading at the right time.

"Well, you asked me to trust you earlier, did you not, my friend?" Najib asked as he smirked at Jonah's answer. Then as Jonah nodded, he continued, *"And I would trust you with my life. So do not worry. I am sure you will like the place I am guiding you to."* That said, Jonah picked up speed and glided the car down the main highway.

Jonah and Najib sat in silence for a while, and as there was no danger for as far as the eye could see, Najib dozed off. This was the time that Jonah took it upon himself to mentally analyze what had happened just a few hours ago. He had been in situations like that before, but there was never a time when he had to protect someone that he truly cared for. Jonah looked to his side and thought about how the man sitting next to him in the passenger seat was a brother to him. He never thought he would come across someone so different from his background and yet proved to be a kindred spirit.

Jonah knew that all he wanted to do that day was protect the Prince and make sure they got out of there in one piece. So, even though they had left behind Abdul and Omar, they knew that the two were the highest-trained officers of Najib's security team, and he never hired anyone he was not a hundred percent sure of - whether it was because of their skill or ability to guard Najib's life.

Chapter 13: The Revelation

As Jonah was in the midst of his thoughts about Omar and Abdul, he felt Najib stir beside him.

"Feeling a little better, eh?" Jonah asked Najib as he sat up in his seat.

"Mhmm... Yeah, I needed that. More than I realized," Najib replied, still a bit groggy from the rest. *"Where are we now?"*

"Well, still a little far from the edge of the city. Maybe like half an hour or so," Jonah replied as he gave a once over at his map.

"Okay, then," Najib added. *"Honestly, Jonah, I cannot wait for us to get to this destination so that we can plan our next move. A lot has been going through my mind. Since the minute I heard those first gunshots, in fact."*

"Like what?" Jonah asked.

"Like the fact that I cannot think to host anything because I will always have a fear of losing either my life or my friends' lives," Najib said as he kept his eyes fixed on the cloudy sky outside his window. The weather had been specifically pleasant that time of year. *"I kept thinking these past couple of hours that this is definitely not the way I wish to live my life. Neither should my friends because God forbid, they begin to question their alliance or friendship with me."*

"Why would anyone regret being your friend, Najib?" Jonah said, never once taking his eyes off the road, but had a rather perplexed expression on his face. *"As far as I know, you have been nothing but generous to every person you have known."*

"Jonah, no matter how generous I am, there will always be some person or some deal that will look more appealing to others," Najib said solemnly. *"There will always be a chance that the culprit behind all this makes his way to one of my allies and attempts to use them and their resources against me."*

Jonah listened to what Najib was saying and thought that his friend was, indeed, correct. The allies and the friendships that Najib had cultivated were powerful and influential people who not only had risky and widespread businesses but were also dangerously protective of their families. This was understandable because, in the business that they were in, it was important and quite customary for them to ensure the protection of all members of their family.

Jonah could see his friend's point of view quite perfectly now. He understood that not only was Najib fearful of the dangers that posed to his friends but to their families as well.

Jonah and Najib were deep in their conversation when they paused and looked straight up the road because a clearing was coming into view. The first thing that caught

Jonah's eye was a tall grey stone boundary wall that presumably went all around the premises and looked like a secret hideout. It was concealed with a wall that was thoroughly lined with barbed wires over the top. The wires had to have been electrical, as the Prince never did anything half-assed.

In the center of the boundary wall, two black iron gates stood tall and wide with a couple of cameras at each top corner. But knowing Najib, Jonah knew that there must have been way more cameras hidden in places than he could even predict. They arrived at the gate, and Najib asked Jonah to roll down his window to speak into the security microphone beside the entrance.

"Um, yes, hello?" Jonah asked into the microphone. *"This is Jonah with Najib."*

Just then, the blank screen above the microphone turned on, and an old man's face came into view. He had thinning hair and looked through a thick set of spectacles. He squinted his eyes and came up close to the screen on his end. Meanwhile, Najib came up close to Jonah's window so that the older man on the other side could see that his boss was indeed in the car, trying to get into the premises of his own free will.

"Salam, Akbar," Najib beckoned at the monitor and microphone. *"I have missed you, dear friend. Open the gate, will you?"*

"Salam, my Prince," Akbar replied. "Of course! Apologies for the delay."

Right then, the main gate opened with a loud screeching sound, indicating that it had not been opened for a long time. As Jonah drove the car into the driveway, the entire structure inside came into view. The structure was a medium-sized bungalow, especially compared to the Prince's main residence. The bungalow was surrounded by an array of flowers in the courtyard, and at the far end was the garage.

Jonah took the car into the garage and parked outside, as it was already filled to the brim with vehicles. He got out of the driver's seat as Najib did the same from the passenger's side. He went around the car and went straight toward Akbar, the man who had opened the gate to the facility. As Jonah was locking up the car, he could see that they both hugged instantly and smiled at each other. Then, he went a little closer.

"Akbar, I cannot wait to hear all about how you have been and how you are keeping up with the place," Najib said as they both moved toward the entrance of the house and then turned around to look at Jonah.

"Jonah, please come in and make yourself at home," Najib yelled out to Jonah. "Akbar's old missus will tell you where to go. So, go freshen up, and I will see you at dinner in a while," he added.

Jonah stood in the middle of the foyer, looking around the house, when he was greeted by an old woman who looked like she was roughly in her late sixties. She adorned a headscarf and loosely covered half of her face. Jonah subtly bowed his head to the woman as she pointed toward the corridor at the far end of the foyer. Jonah took the hint and followed her to a guest room that had already been picked out for him.

The decor of the bungalow was quite similar to that of Najib's main residence within the city, but this place looked and felt more like a safe house. In his long line of work, Jonah was accustomed to smelling gunpowder from a mile off, and he could certainly smell that the place was packed with arsenal. He just could not see all of it. Although Jonah had spotted some of the guns displayed in cabinets in a small pathway on one end of the foyer, he knew that there had to be more guns stored in this place if he were to simply follow that pathway.

Jonah quietly made his way to the room picked out for him; entering the room, he thanked the old woman. She bowed her head in return and then left. After closing the door, Jonah removed his jacket and thought that he needed a change of clothes and a shower. It felt like it had been ages since he had worn a clean set of clothes. The entire ordeal with the auction had made it seem like Jonah had truly been through days without changing. He opened the armoire near the bathroom, and lo and behold, there was a pair of jeans and a black t-shirt folded inside and a clean pair of socks and combat boots at the bottom.

Jonah looked at the things inside the armoire, seemingly waiting for him, and smiled to himself. He figured that the Prince must have made the call early on when Jonah was busy looking at ways to get them both to the safe house in one piece. Jonah grabbed the clothes and went to the bathroom to take a shower. Standing under the water, he felt all the exhaustion and fatigue wash away. After a long and relaxing shower, he went back to the room and was drying his hair when he heard a knock at the door.

"Yes?" he called out instead of opening the door.

"Sir, this is Akbar. Master Najib would like you to join him for dinner in the dining area," Akbar said from the other end of the door.

"Alright, then. Please tell him I will be right there," Jonah replied.

Jonah finished dressing up and then made his way out of the room and toward the dining room. It was not hard to find, as he could see it when standing in the middle of the foyer. As he made it to the dining table, Jonah could see Najib already sitting at the head of the table and folding his napkin onto his lap.

"Oh, good, you are here right on time, Jonah. Take a seat and let's dig in," Najib said as Jonah took his seat at the right hand

of the head seat. *"All that we have to talk about will seem much more reasonable after we have had some food in our bellies."*

Jonah nodded, folded his napkin onto his lap, and just then, Akbar and his wife brought over two fully stacked plates of food.

"So, what do you think of this safe house, Jonah?" Najib asked as they both dug into the food. *"Ooh, this is delicious, Akbar. Do give my compliments to the misses, please."* Akbar simply bowed his head in return and left the room.

"I think it suits you quite well, Najib. You do have an eye to keep things in shape and just how they should be," Jonah replied.

"Thank you, my friend." Najib continued, *"This abode is quite precious to my heart, even if I never thought I would have to use it. You see, there are only four people apart from Akbar and his wife who can access it any time they want, and two of them are sitting at this dinner table."*

Then judging by the confused expression on Jonah's face, Najib continued. *"The other two are, of course, Omar and Abdul. Now, I understand the gravity of the situation as we wait with bated breath for those two to come back unharmed. Well, almost."*

"I am sure that they will come back in one piece, knowing how well they have been trained," Jonah said as he enjoyed every bite of his delicious food. He hadn't realized just how hungry he was until he dug into that plate.

"I agree with you, Jonah. I have complete faith in their capabilities." Najib continued as he finished his food, *"But I do have to tell you something. I am in touch with some of the most prominent figures of the Saudi armed forces. Not only that, but I know people in the underground regimes of intelligence forces."*

"I am aware of that, Najib. Why are you telling me this suddenly?" Jonah questioned as he, too, was now done with his food.

"I am telling you this because have you not wondered why any of those people were not called when we were under attack back at the auction venue?" Najib asked, and Jonah continued to appear confused, as he genuinely was.

"The reason for that is, Jonah, that I intentionally had to let it happen. I know you might think it to be rather extreme, but it was the only way that I could kill two birds with one stone. I wanted to get rid of the one traitor amongst the entirety of my security crew," Najib admittedly said to Jonah as he leaned back in his chair.

Jonah's eyes widened as he tried to understand the implication of this revelation. He leaned back in his chair and stared at the now-empty plate in front of him. The Prince had intentionally let his men die to get rid of one traitor.

Chapter 14: Afraid

Najib could tell by the look on his friend's face that Jonah was having a hard time coming to terms with what he had just revealed to him, so he explained further.

"You do understand that this would have been the only way to get rid of the traitor, right? Any other way would have made things way riskier than they already are," Najib said. *"If, say, there was only one traitor among the ranks conversing with the enemy, I could not predict who else was safeguarding that main traitor as well. The chain would have gone on and on with no end, with me trying to get to the bottom of the situation. I do not know if they could have foreseen this outcome or not, but they signed their own death warrant as soon as they made the decision to betray me."*

The Prince then continued and said, *"I have paid them to be loyal. But if I cannot trust the guards who are meant to protect me, then what is the point of having them at all?"*

As soon as Jonah heard the Prince's reasoning, he could understand just why this had been the only way for him to fish out the bad seeds among the guards. Any other method could have made Najib more vulnerable than he already was because the guards could have planned a mutiny for all he knew.

"Najib, just when I think you cannot surprise me anymore, you do." Jonah sat up in his chair and said to Najib, *"I cannot say that I could have come up with the same solution as you did. But then again, I am not in the same position as you, so I can merely empathize. But my friend, I know how generous you were to your employees from the very beginning. From paying for their livelihood to rescuing them from obscurity, you did it all. So, to come face to face with a decision like that, I can say that I do not envy you, my friend. But I do respect you."*

"I appreciate you saying that Jonah," Najib said. *"Of all people, I knew you would understand my position, and that is why you are the closest person I have in my life."*

As they were coming to a close with their conversation, Najib and Jonah heard a car pulling up outside the front gates. They both knew who that could be, so they instinctually looked at each other and rushed up from their chairs. Then as they went out into the courtyard, they could see the vehicle come to a stop outside the garage and park beside Jonah's car. Akbar closed the gate behind them, and Abdul and Omar both got out of the vehicle with multiple wounds on their arms and legs, looking defeated but proud.

Najib waved at them with one hand to come inside and put the other hand on Jonah's shoulder. They all looked at each other with bittersweet smiles on their faces that portrayed a subtle sense of victory. They all knew that the next few hours would be spent briefing them about the ordeal that Jonah and Najib had left behind, so they went inside and looked forward to planning their next move.

***

Jonah stood in the driveway and hugged Najib for the last time, for the foreseeable future at least, let go, and said, "Why do I feel like it is going to be quite some time before I see you again, my friend? I mean, I know that with the kind of lives we both lead, it won't be long before we come together, but somehow, I wish for something different today."

"And what is that my friend?" Najib asked.

"That maybe it is not best for me to go away right now, or that I would worry less about your safety at the end of the day if I stay here and not at the safe house you have picked out for me," Jonah replied as he leaned against the blue mustang behind him.

Najib then smiled, placed a hand on Jonah's shoulder, and said, "Jonah, I am honored to have a friend that worries for me. Truly. But you have your own life to live, and I have other engagements that I must take care of. Besides, I have Abdul and Omar here with me, so you do not have to worry about my safety. I will be okay. However, what I can say for certain is that we will see each other again very soon to figure out the bulk of our plan. For now, live your life. While residing in the safe house, of course."

"Very well," Jonah said. "I will see you when I see you, Najib. Stay safe."

"Same goes for you, Jonah," Najib added as he watched Jonah slide into the backseat of the car. "Oh, and Jonah?"

"What?" Jonah answered.

"The car is yours. Call it a parting gift. Partially," Najib called out. "Or maybe a token of my thanks for being by my side."

Too stunned to speak, Jonah merely had a perplexed look on his face. Then he asked as he gestured toward the driver, "Najib, then what do you suppose this gentleman at the front will be doing when he drops me off?"

"His name is Hakim. He will be your bodyguard after he takes you to the safe house. Honestly, Jonah, you may call me selfish for this, but there is a chip and a direct radio line planted inside the mustang's mechanism. So if God forbid, something bad happens, I will know. You will be able to let me know."

"Najib...just... thank you," Jonah somberly replied.

"You're very welcome," Najib continued. "Now leave before I change my mind." A smirk played on Najib's face as he waved goodbye to Jonah. By the end of the conversation, Jonah knew that no matter what happened, he had someone always ready to be by his side, and the same was the case with Jonah as well. He would use all his knowledge and strength to catch the culprit behind all this strife.

***

As Jonah reached the safe house Najib had picked out for him, he was reminded of the sentence Abdul uttered after returning from the auction venue. He had simply mentioned that they had to blow up the entire venue so not a single adversary that they might have missed could escape. After they both found refuge for a while in an office at the venue, Abdul and Omar discovered secret passages that were beyond the enemies' reach. Those passages had not only led the guests out but proved to be the escape route for Abdul and Omar. So as it turned out, the exchange of fire was mainly between Najib's men and the attackers.

Jonah recalled that as Abdul and Omar were seated on the living room sofa and filling Najib in on the details, the entire story proved that the man behind the attack was relentless. His attack dogs would have stopped at nothing to get to the Prince. So, the only option left for them was to blow the entire venue to the ground so that there was no one left alive to carry on the hunt for the Prince.

Jonah had listened intently to every single detail that Omar and Abdul were telling them, and he buried his head in both hands as he leaned on the living room window.

"How many lives are going to be lost in this crusade?" Jonah turned and exclaimed. Thoughts were circling his mind of all the people killed simply because a Prince was rumored to be in a place. It didn't sit well with him that he knew about a genocide that nobody in history would even talk about. Then he thought of all the genocides that never saw the light of day because of similar situations.

"Jonah... My friend, I know just how you are feeling at this moment," Najib said as he placed a hand on Jonah's shoulder. "Believe me. There was always a chance that this crusade, as you put it, was going to turn uglier. The man behind this is acting nothing less than a hunter and a relentless one at that."

Then Najib put his hand to his heart and said, "I have lost people that I cared about, but I do not plan on losing anyone anymore. But make no mistake. I will not rest until that man is six feet under. This man will stop at nothing to get a hold of me or my loved ones, which is exactly why I have just the right place for you, Jonah."

That was when Najib told Jonah of the safe house he had picked out for his friend; he knew that after this incident, Jonah's house would no longer be safe. So, when Jonah arrived at this new hideout, it was nothing short of Najib's standards. Only that it was somewhat smaller than the one Najib was staying at, which was perfect for Jonah because the lavish lifestyle was not exactly to his taste. The safe house came with its own shooting range and a fully equipped gym to keep Jonah occupied with the necessities.

As he rummaged through clothes to wear, Jonah was reminded of the Prince's promise of seeing him again soon enough. He knew it wouldn't be for auctions this time, as the Prince counted him as one of his most trusted friends. Being close to Prince meant attracting the kind of attention no ordinary man would want to attract, and he was reminded of this every moment that he spent with Najib.

Nevertheless, he would not change this for anything else offered. In the hideout he was in now, Jonah could begin to harness his skills even more. There was a chance that he could learn from Hakim whatever he could offer. So that is exactly what he attempted.

Jonah woke up for his regular exercise and training session that he had never missed ever since he had figured out that it was something that he loved. He knocked on Hakim's door and said, "Morn'in', old man."

Hakim opened the door with a scrunched face while rubbing his eye with one hand.

"I know, I know, you ain't that old, but hey, I was wondering if you wanted to join me on my run. It would halfway be around the premises and then a little out the boundary wall."

"Hm... Well, I guess it would not kill me," Hakim agreed.

Chapter 15: The Safehouse

At the safe house, Jonah woke up earlier than usual—something about sleeping in an unfamiliar house. He was uneasy from the start and was not quite sure when he would become familiar with these new routines or even the safe house. It was all a bit of a blur for Jonah— to say the least. He could not begin to shake the feeling that things would not become so unfamiliar soon.

So, with that sentiment of uneasiness, Jonah got ready for his morning run, knowing that Hakim would join him soon when he woke up. As Jonah came out to the small courtyard, he stood still and saw someone he had known a long time ago. A black Jaguar was parked just at the edge of the driveway, and a woman with those memorable long legs stood leaning beside the driving edge of the car door.

It was Nadia. Not only was she an ex-love interest for Jonah, but she was quite capable with her hands when it came to weapons and close-range combat. She looked like she had not aged a day in the last few years that he hadn't seen her. Whereas if Jonah looked in the mirror a few times a day, he could see the past laid out in terms of a few dark circles underneath his eyes.

Seeing Nadia appear in the safe house and looking just as divine as ever was obviously Najib's doing. He knew what Jonah needed to take the edge off from the past few days of turmoil and gunfights.

"Why, hello, Nadia. What brings you to my temporary humble abode?" Jonah asked Nadia.

"Hello to you too, Jonah," Nadia replied without moving from her leaned-back position. *"Najib gave me a call and said that you needed me to be here."*

"And you just arrived?" Jonah questioned. *"Weren't you meant to be detailing as security for a certain first lady at this time of year?"*

"Dammit. I completely forgot about that. Oh, well! I guess I just was not in the mood to go," Nadia quipped. Her sarcasm was as vibrant as ever.

Jonah smiled and then sighed in return. *"I must be honest, Nadia. These last few days have been weird as all hell. I just cannot keep myself from thinking about all the lives that have been lost because of all this."*

"I know," Nadia replied. *"Najib filled me in with all the latest updates on the case. He knew that you would need someone to talk to about all this, and it was not going to be the burly security guard he sent with you."*

"Oh, Hakim is a good guy, and he is good at his job, but he isn't much of a talker," Jonah added. *"I wanted to share my thoughts about what happened and what I feel is the solution*

for all this. I just don't know whether I would be able to put my spin on it as much as I would have liked to."

"What do you mean?" Nadia asked.

"Nadia, I care about Najib, and I understand why he needed to be so secretive about the whole thing. But I have known him for years. I feel as though if only I had known about this entire ordeal a lot earlier, I could have done more, and maybe all those lives at the auction wouldn't have been lost," Jonah said dejectedly.

Nadia touched Jonah's shoulder somberly and said, *"I can understand how you feel, and what you wish for is completely valid. But, Jonah, you said it yourself. You have known Najib for a long time, and by now, you must understand that what he values most of all is this air of mystery and intrigue. Now, it has led to a lot of mishaps between a lot of people. Yourself included. But he cannot be changed. Especially after the things he has gone through. And to be honest, I can relate."*

Jonah bowed his head for a moment and contemplated where Nadia was coming from. She had a tumultuous childhood that led to her fleeing her family home and becoming someone who was more in control of her life.

When Nadia saw Jonah visibly take a sigh of relief, she suggested that they move this conversation indoors.

Jonah agreed and gave up on his morning run, just that one time. He knew that with Nadia's sudden arrival, things would not seem so clouded after all. Jonah stood up straight, extended his hand to Nadia, and walked to Jonah's room together. This reunion was not only much needed for both Jonah and Nadia equally, but it happened at the perfect relaxation point where they would simply not be disturbed by anyone or any matter.

Arriving at Jonah's bedroom, Nadia closed the door and locked it. Turning to Jonah, she forcibly pushed him on the bed, slamming her lips to his with the fury of wild passion. The distant time they had faced while they were both off doing their duty was enough to ignite enough passion for them to skip the foreplay. Well, almost.

Nadia quickly undressed Jonah, pulling his pants down. She grabbed his member and whispered softly in his ear, *"Damn, I missed you."* Nadia always knew what she was doing, and Jonah could not have loved it more. The kind of bond they had was one with no strings attached, with sexual chemistry never being off the table. So that evening, passion rose to the highest level anyone could only imagine.

The next few days that followed were of pure bliss. They knew that what they needed most at that point in time was each other's company and a shoulder to share where they were in their lives. One day, as Jonah took Nadia with him for his regular morning run, he explained to her that even though the head honcho behind the targeted attacks on Najib and his alliances was unknown, they had a significant idea of how he could attack and where those places could be.

Since Nadia had her own expertise in matters like that, she suggested in every instance that the Prince would travel to his mostly publicized engagements. Jonah was meant to travel with him. "*It does not matter how many people he has with him or those guys, Abdul and Omar; you are going with him whether he asks for it or not,*" Nadia said to Jonah as they briskly walked around the land. "*Ever since you have told me that Najib suspected mutiny within his ranks, I somehow do not trust Abdul and Omar as well. Not until the culprit is caught, at least.*"

Jonah nodded in response, as he knew that Nadia and her intuitions as of yet had never been proven wrong. So, he would do well to heed her guidance and wait till things settled a bit to decide whether Abdul and Omar were truly on their side.

The respite enjoyed by Jonah and Nadia proved to be short-lived as Najib walked in, with Abdul and Omar in tow, just as they were about to head in for a shower after the morning run.

"*Aah, I see you got my present, my friend,*" Najib yelled out to Jonah as he was about to go indoors with Nadia, hand in hand.

Jonah turned around and smiled ear to ear to see his friend healthy and safe. *"Najib!"* Jonah exclaimed as they both hugged and greeted each other. *"Man am I glad to see you. How was the trip?"* He then diverted his attention to Abdul and Omar. *"Hello to you both as well. I see that you're recovering nicely from your wounds."*

"We're all doing well, Jonah, and I see that you, too, look healthy and relaxed here," Najib replied as he looked between Nadia and Jonah.

"What can we say? Never better," Nadia added.

"I am glad," Najib said as he walked indoors with Jonah and the others by his side. *"I do have to say, though. Nadia, I am sorry, dear, but there is something very important I need to discuss with Jonah, and for that, you will have to excuse us."*

"Of course. I do not mind," Nadia answered. She then swiftly turned around and walked to Jonah's room.

Najib bowed his head slightly in gratitude and sat on the living room sofa, with Abdul and Omar sitting on the opposite one. He then addressed Jonah as he asked him to sit beside him. *"Jonah, my friend, the deal I am about to offer you is going to be a dangerous one but also the biggest one of your life. I want to offer you a way out of this mess because I have seen how much this has taken a toll on your mental health. That is why I want you to help me get rid of my biggest enemy."*

"But Najib, isn't that what we are meant to do anyway?" Jonah asked.

"It is, but that is only half of the deal," Najib added and saw the perplexed look on Jonah's face. *"The other half of the deal is that you shall not be asked for any other mission, ever, after this one is done."*

"What do you mean?" Jonah asked, perplexed.

"Jonah, I know that you have been meaning to leave this lifestyle behind for quite some time now. So, I have made a few arrangements, and the organization you have been part of for these kinds of operations will no longer bug you if you wish to live a quiet life here or anywhere, for that matter. Whether with Nadia or by yourself, it is up to you. You can retire now," Najib told him.

Jonah was indeed tempted, as he wanted nothing more than to leave this lifestyle behind already. But the price made him take pause. The excitement of the entire adventure was amazing, and he totally enjoyed all the experiences. So, he just could not decide whether that was what he wanted anymore.

Chapter 16: The Plan

Jonah sat back on the sofa, contemplating what Najib had just told him. According to him, the plan he was about to tell everyone would prove valuable for the entire team and not just Najib's safety. For as long as Jonah had known the Prince, he was always a fan of dramatics, and he simply could not do any task without adding a level of certain flare to the affair. But judging by what he had said, for now, the plan would be simple enough for Jonah to agree with.

"My plan for getting the enemy is nothing too excessive or elaborate," Najib said as he kept reading the perplexed expressions on Jonah's face. *"The reason for that is that there is one thing I would hate to be, and that is predictable."*

"I understand that you need me to help you with whatever you have going on in that head of yours, but explain everything to me in detail if I am meant to put my life in danger again," Jonah replied, leaning a little forward. *"Najib, you are like a brother to me, but you have to admit that what we have planned or done so far to get to the bottom of who is behind all this and what his motives are, has not worked. So, what makes you so sure that this new plan will?"* he continued.

Najib took a moment to figure out how he would respond to Jonah. There must be a way for Jonah to let go of any inhibitions gathered in him. Especially after he had met Nadia, there was a big part of Jonah that wanted a simple life with a regular job and family. Najib had watched Jonah closely for the past few weeks and observed that his friend was now at a point in his life where he just wanted to be carefree and live a normal life away from the chaos and bloodshed.

"Jonah, my friend, and brother, ever since you have been in this safehouse, I can see how happy you seem to be away from that life of danger and intrigue," Najib answered. He took a pause before continuing, *"I also understand that even though elements of a person's previous life do not leave his mind, there is a huge part of your heart that yearns to have what other normal people do. So, trust me, I can see that same yearning in your eyes."*

"Honestly, I am not surprised that you do. I know you to be highly perceptive, Najib. So go on. Tell me the rest of your masterful plan," Jonah added.

As soon as Jonah uttered that last sentence, a smile spread across Najib's face, and he knew that if Jonah had asked for the plan to be revealed, then that meant he was in for the whole thing. Najib knew that if Jonah was least bothered about what his friend was planning to do for his adversary, then he would have straight-up said, "No."

Jonah was the kind of person who either went all in or did not bother to be included in any way. So, this time, Najib simply nodded his head with a smile and asked Abdul to bring over a roller case that presumably contained a large amount of paperwork.

Jonah, on the other hand, was thinking about something that had been circling his mind every time he went for his morning runs. He knew that simply being the Prince's right hand would forfeit his life. However, ever since Najib became a whole lot more honest with Jonah about who his enemy's targets were and how he felt that he needed to exact revenge, Jonah had been more open to assisting the Prince with his recent endeavors. He was ready to risk it all to get out of this mess.

Jonah knew that as long as he was associated with the Prince, his life would be in danger. So, he thought maybe getting his friend out of mortal danger might prove to be the greatest adventure of his life. Therefore, when Najib said that the idea was simple - lure the prey out and murder him in broad daylight - Jonah knew that before anything would pan out, this agreement was literally already signed in blood.

Najib took the roller case and opened it to reveal a bunch of maps and blueprints of some sort. With Abdul and Omar's help, the maps were spread out over the big coffee table in the living room.

"These are the blueprints for our adversary's compound," Najib said nonchalantly as he sat straight up on the sofa.

Jonah's eyes shot up at Najib and stayed wide open. He then looked between Omar and Abdul, and they both nodded to confirm that they had indeed gotten a hold of these blueprints themselves.

"H... How?" Jonah asked as he just could not believe what he was seeing. A million questions had been running through his mind, but all that he could muster to ask was that single word.

Then Najib proceeded to roll up his sleeves and tell Jonah about how he and his men got a hold of the layouts. Najib told Jonah that the task had been brewing in his mind ever since that day at the auction. He had been thinking about infiltrating the enemy from the inside out and keeping tabs on him to get to the bottom of his schemes.

Najib wanted to know just how much was under the adversary's control regarding an arsenal and manpower so that he knew just what kind of beast he would be dealing with. The question was, who could he pick that the adversary, or his men had not yet encountered? Najib told Jonah that as soon as he spent a day at his safehouse after returning from the auction fiasco, he realized that there was someone who he trusted and who was smart enough to get behind the enemy line without any supervision or arousing any suspicion.

"Tobias," Najib said as he raised his eyebrows.

"Your butler?" Jonah asked, almost dumbfounded. *"What experience does he have with this kind of operation? Also, how could you be so sure, Najib, that he would not be working with your enemy in the first place?"*

"Honestly, Jonah, I must admit that I was not quite sure. But since I had exhausted all my other options and was not willing to lose any more of my men, friends, or allies, that was my best bet," Najib answered. *"Therefore, I had a deep conversation with Tobias, and so did Omar and Abdul. We all talked for a few hours at the safehouse with zero disturbance and even though I do not have a lair filled with a top-of-the-line armory, what I do have are resources."*

"That is all well and good, Najib, but we are still not considering the fact that the man is not a trained spy or even an agent like Omar or Abdul," Jonah said.

"Agreed, so why not use this fact to our advantage?" Najib tried to reason with Jonah. *"I realized that sending Tobias into the proverbial lion's den would be risky, and so I raised this honest point to the man, and he said something in return that almost led me to believe him wholeheartedly, even though that was going to come soon enough."*

Najib knew that would grab Jonah's attention, which it did.

Chapter 17: The Execution

"What? What did he say?" Jonah questioned.

"Tobias said that he had been waiting patiently but also anxiously to prove himself to me," Najib said. "He told me that he had heard from some of the security guys that I did not fully trust the team I had carried with me for a long time, especially after the attacks. Therefore, he was all too willing to act as a potential employee for the enemy and act as a butler for as long as possible so he could get a hold of something at their compound for us to use."

"Wow. I must say that he is braver than I thought," Jonah said.

"He really proved to be, Jonah," Najib continued. "Within a week, Tobias grew his beard and colored it. He made himself look like an immigrant foreigner who was looking for a job. So, he went to their doorstep acting like it and claimed that someone in town had referred him. This was true because some of the staff at that compound had been advertising for a butler and cook. So, Tobias went in, cooked a few things for them, and was instantly hired. That same weekend, he snuck into an office at the place, grabbed these, and left."

"So, you mean to tell me that you wish to infiltrate the place?" Jonah asked.

"I thought that could be the initial plan, but of course, I soon realized that it was just not me," Najib answered. "That is not how I would do things, and why would I step onto his turf when I can easily bring him to mine? So, what these blueprints have done is given me a better idea of who this person is, even if I have no plans of going to him to find that out."

"What? Who is it?" Jonah blurted out.

"My cousin, Habib Al-Jabbar," Najib said in a solemn tone, almost looking down at his feet with his hands held together. It looked as if this was the thing, he had been most embarrassed to admit in his whole life. "I understand that it is normal in my culture to have blood-thirsty relatives, but this man has taken his envy way too far. He is the son of my eldest uncle, my father's brother."

"I... I just don't know what to say, Najib. This is wild!" Jonah whispered. "I mean, what the hell? I just cannot believe it!"

"Jonah, Habib's father was the most cut-throat businessman of the family, and according to his theory, the only way to do business and make it well known in the world was through fear," Najib said. "My uncle was famous within the family and the extended circles as the man who just changed into this monster after his wife died. So, he trained his son to grow up as the nastiest version of himself. All that he could not accomplish, his son did."

"So, what does his envy have to do with you and your allies?" Jonah asked, constantly perplexed at this entire topic of the Prince's cousin being the man behind all the attacks on his close friends and allies.

"The only logical explanation I can give you for that question is that Habib has always been an envious individual. He could not stand the fact that my father had progressed as a businessman while leading the charge of his employees with kindness. My father, God rest his soul, taught me that the business world is about studying people instead of invoking fear within them. Habib apparently could not stand the fact that his cousin was doing a lot better and earning not just the respect of the business tycoons of the world but also their monetary support," Najib replied.

"This is hard to process, honestly. I know that family can be harsher than the outside world, but this takes the cake. Najib, that man is responsible for the murder of so many people at that auction! Not to mention injuring so many of your friends," Jonah said as he got up from his sofa and started slowly pacing the room.

Najib got up from the sofa and came to stand next to Jonah. "My friend, I understand your anger and confusion. But to remedy that, you must listen to the whole plan I have devised with Abdul and Omar."

"Trust us, Jonah. It going to be one hell of a final showdown," Abdul spoke up. He had not moved from his seat the entire time they had been in that room. Omar, on the other hand, had gotten up to get drinks from the kitchen. It always seemed a little unsettling to Jonah that these two men, Abdul, and Omar, always kept their cool around intense situations or conversations. While Jonah had been freaking out over the fact that first, Najib sent his butler into the lion's den and then found out that it was his cousin who had been behind all this the whole time, the two just kept straight faces.

Najib's plan was simple. He explained each step one by one and paced around the room while talking enthusiastically about the fact that he had come up with it mostly by himself. He wanted to arrange an auction from a third-party point of view, meaning that the orchestrator of the auction would be someone other than the Prince - at least, that was what the marketing strategy would act as. The focal object of that auction would be something Najib's cousin wouldn't be able to resist. So, when Habib would join the auction and proceeded to position himself as a guest within the audience, that would be enough time for Omar and Abdul to set a bomb in his car.

As Najib laid out this first part of his plan, Jonah understood what he meant earlier when he said Najib wanted the adversary to be incriminated on his turf. Najib wanted to orchestrate a scenario where he would be in charge and control the entire operation without ever coming into the picture. With the help of this plan, the Prince would not only get a hold of his enemy but also stay in control the whole time with his team around him.

This is also where Jonah would come in. Najib explained further that Jonah would have to elongate the auction as much as possible so it would give Abdul and Omar enough time to quietly take down any armed guards that Habib would have arrived with at the auction venue. The guns, he said, would be equipped with silencers, and therefore, no one would hear a peep from the outside.

While the plan seemed foolproof, it would not be easy to have Jonah be the auctioneer as his face would be well-known to his adversary and the guests by that point. So, they would have to do it in a way that nobody found out that Jonah had stepped onto the auction stage. They all instantly looked at each other and understood that Jonah's appearance would need to be changed, almost to the extent that no matter who came up close to him, they would not figure out that it was Jonah.

By the time the plan had been thoroughly explained to Jonah, Najib merely asked one question from his dear friend. "So, can I count you in? For the final time?"

"Najib, you are the only person who knows just how much I want to avoid any more bloodshed. So, even though I know that more blood will need to be spilled for this to end, I cannot say no to your plan. At least that way, I will know what I am going to be responsible for," Jonah replied calmly. He had become resolute in his decision from that point on.

Najib hugged him instantly and said, "Come then, my friend. We will return to the palace to prepare."

In Jonah's eyes, the agreement felt like it had already been signed in blood. No matter how much he tried to convince himself that the Prince would be better off without his assistance and that he did not need to be part of another mission, he could feel the pressure in his bones. He knew that he simply could not step away from the final showdown of this entire affair, and more so, he would not be able to live with himself if something horrific happened to the Prince and he was not there to lend protection.

If anything, the thought that it would be over soon and Najib's adversary would be caught inside a foolproof plan was enough to motivate Jonah and seal the decision in his mind. It took Jonah a few minutes to gather up his things and pack them all up. After he was done, he said his goodbyes to Nadia.

Nadia stood at the car porch and waved goodbye to Jonah as he sat in the car. Najib, Jonah, Abdul, and Omar left the safehouse and embarked on their trip to the Prince's palace.

Chapter 18: Deteriorating

The four men, Najib, Jonah, Abdul, and Omar, had decided to take the shortcut to the palace. As it was going to become the base for what they were planning, they needed to get there as soon as possible. The car ride had been swift, and their journey had been smooth, considering that they traveled in the middle of winter in Egypt. The weather was notoriously unsettling in the region during that time of the year. Even though they were prepared to encounter surprise rainfall or winds during their journey, the men decided that the shortcut would be the best option, just in case.

As soon as they all arrived at the palace, they were greeted by Tobias, who was waiting for them in the courtyard. Najib got out of the car first and shook his butler's hand. *"Hello, there, Tobias. Settling in well, I assume?"* Najib asked.

"Of course, my Prince," Tobias replied. *"It was like I never left."*

Jonah also got out of the car and grabbed his suitcase from the trunk while Omar and Abdul did the same, except they grabbed Najib's luggage as well. Holding his suitcase in one hand, Jonah came up and hugged Tobias with his other arm. *"Hope you're doing well, Tobias. I must say we have to toast your latest and brave endeavors. I kind of feel proud, even though I did not train you for the mission,"* Jonah said as he made his way inside the palace foyer.

"I appreciate that. Thank you, Mr. Jonah," Tobias replied.

Everyone went inside the palace, and the first thing each of them could think of was to freshen up and get straight to planning out the details. After a short while, everyone gathered in Najib's study, and as soon as they were all inside, Omar stood in the doorway and told Tobias not to disturb the room until one of the men inside opened the door themselves. The butler understood that the meeting should not be disturbed and left the room immediately after placing a tray of water and goblets at the far end of the room.

Jonah watched as Najib and the other two spread out the blueprints of the venue Najib had selected for the auction. Meanwhile, Abdul opened up a projector screen to reveal that he had planned a layout of where these four men were to be importantly placed. *"As far as I can see, Najib, it appears that you three have basically panned out where everyone and everything is going to go,"* Jonah muttered at Najib as he placed a weight on the edge of the map on the table. *"The question is, where exactly do you want me to be?"*

"Jonah, since when have you doubted your involvement in a mission like this?" Najib questioned. *"You are the most lethal sharpshooter I know. Not only will you be disguised to look like someone else, I believe it will be you who takes out my enemy."*

Confusion took over Jonah's face as he went speechless for a spell. *"I'm flattered, Najib, but my friend, he is your enemy. Haven't you at least wanted to put a bullet in the guy's head yourself?"* Jonah asked.

"Listen, it would be ideal for me to do so, but I am afraid I have to admit that as much as I have practiced for this day all my life, no one can make a shot like you can, Jonah," Najib added. *"Just face it, you are gifted, my friend. So, the moment I point him out to you in the crowd, through an earpiece, of course, you will take the shot."*

Jonah simply nodded, and they all carried on with the plan to hash out where each man would be placed at the venue. Najib worked his way through his allies and produced a perfectly good cover auction in some time. He knew just who would be interested in joining the auction and that they would not question his motives twice if he simply told them that the theme he planned for this auction, in particular, would be a masquerade.

"Why masquerade?" Jonah asked.

"The reason is simple. Each guest will be one of my acquaintances or an enemy of my cousin, Habib. So, I thought, what better way to have the right audience for this?" Najib answered nonchalantly. *"The enemy of my enemy is my friend. Plus, to keep their identities secret for as long as possible, I figured that a masquerade would be the best option."*

Jonah was honestly surprised at the elaborate thought process Najib had gone through in order to bring his enemy to their knees. After deciding on the venue and order in which Abdul and Omar would be positioned outside the venue and away from the eyes of Najib's allies and especially his enemy, the date for the auction and valuable artifact were also confirmed.

"There is a rare pink diamond that Habib's father had his eye on for as long as I can remember," Najib said as he gave his reasoning for selecting the artifact for this particular auction. *"As far as my father could tell me what that jealousy was for, he said that he wanted to buy it for his wife, but before he could get his hands on it, my father had already purchased it for my mother. The diamond is the last one left in the world, and it just so happens that it is an heirloom from my father and mother to me. Now, I do not know when I will take a wife or even if I will. But, one thing is for sure, I would rather give it to a worthy friend than that insolent fool of a cousin."*

"Understood," Jonah replied. *"And since you will stay hidden while watching everything from the camera monitors, will I be guarding the diamond as well?"*

"I suppose, yes, my friend," Najib answered. *"Would that be okay for you?"*

Jonah nodded and gave Najib an expression that indicated he would be up for the job, but of course, inside, he was sweating bullets. After the story Najib had just told them about the diamond, Jonah knew that he would have to be on his A game, at least until Omar and Abdul got inside the venue after taking care of the guards outside. The plan was set, and the timeline was laid. Jonah and Najib determined that they were finally ready for the kill, and with that, they decided to open the doors to the palace study room.

Tobias stood outside the room and waited to escort the Prince to his bedroom with a cup of steaming hot coffee in hand. *"I shall see you men in the morning. Get some rest,"* Najib said as he turned to head to his room up the stairs.

As the big judgment day drew close, Jonah noticed something off about the Prince's health. He noticed that Najib had been eating properly, but he would also get sick straight after the meal. This led to the palace staff completely changing his menu to see what he had gotten this seemingly horrifying reaction from. Najib's family doctor was instantly called to the palace to figure out what had gotten into the Prince's system all of a sudden. However, he simply could not figure out what was wrong.

On top of that, Najib was stubborn enough to claim that this was merely stomach flu and that they all had nothing to worry about. On the other hand, Jonah could not help but notice that Najib's health had slowly started deteriorating. It started from the vomits but gradually led to little coughs here and there. Soon, Najib was evidently having full-blown coughs and fits.

Once, during breakfast, Jonah decided to join Najib in his room and to keep him company as they chatted over sharing more of Najib's family history. This was Jonah's attempt to get his friend's mind off the sudden deterioration of his health. Everyone in the palace had been confused and worried, but Jonah had been the only one who kept a solid focus on having his friend get better so that he could exact the revenge he so dearly wanted. However, right after breakfast, Najib looked like he was about to have another fit of coughing, so instead of ringing someone, Jonah took Najib to the bathroom and helped him.

As Najib coughed that day, Jonah could clearly see that there were splatters of blood all over the sink. The worry in Jonah's mind increased tenfold, and it was at that moment that he decided to take matters into his own hands. He simply could not trust anyone at the palace when it came to saving Najib's health. So, after bringing his friend back to his room and helping him onto the bed, Jonah said, *"The plan is getting postponed for a while. Just for now, Najib. You need your rest and not worry because neither of us is going anywhere. So, the plan will continue when you get better."*

Jonah left Najib to rest and left his bedroom. After taking a few paces down the stairs, he saw Tobias leaving the kitchen. Jonah caught up with Tobias, and in a whispered tone, he said, *"I need your help, Tobias. I am worried for the Prince and know that you are as well."*

Tobias simply nodded and listened quietly to Jonah.

Chapter 19: The Obvious

Jonah took Tobias into the kitchen nearby and closed the door behind him. He then made sure that all the windows were shut completely in order to have a thorough conversation without the fear of someone listening in. Jonah went up to each window above the sinks to make sure that they were closed. The whole time, Tobias maintained a bewildered expression on his face as he had never seen Jonah this on edge before.

"Umm, sir? Should I be worried more? I mean, for something other than his highness fighting for his life now?" Tobias asked as he watched Jonah pace around the kitchen while clutching his hair. Tobias could see the small beads of sweat starting to form on his forehead when he came to a stop in front of the butler.

"Tobias, whatever I say to you in this instant, I expect it will be kept secret, even from Najib, at least until I say so," Jonah replied.

"You have my word, sir. I trust that you have the Prince's best interest at heart," Tobias said, nodding his head in affirmation.

"Good, that is what I wanted to hear. I must tell you that I have this sneaking suspicion that Najib has been poisoned," Jonah continued, and when he saw the colors of the butler's

face change, he added, *"Now, I know what you must be thinking. How can he be poisoned when the food gets tasted by Abdul before Najib even takes a bite...."*

"That is exactly what I am thinking," Tobias uttered. *"You know the half of it, sir. I say that because I am the one who oversees every single step of the cooking process inside the kitchen, and I see when the groceries are brought in. Not only that, but I taste the food before even Abdul gets a chance to taste it."*

Jonah was stunned at the lengthy process each person in Najib's palace had to go through in order to achieve the Prince's safety. He paced around his side of the kitchen and ran his hands through his hair multiple times. The confusion and multiple scenarios his mind was going through were not getting him close to any conclusion.

Jonah used to think that someone inside the Prince's ranks had it out for him and that they were double-crossing him to the point where he would eventually get killed. But poisoning the food just did not make sense as there were way too many variables involved. However, Jonah was determined to find the answers to this horrific situation before anyone other than Tobias could find out or even before Najib's health deteriorated any further.

"One of these days, I will find the answer, and I shall do it before my best friend falls prey to such a malicious and lowlife scheme to end him," Jonah said to Tobias and left the kitchen.

In the following days, while keeping a close eye on Najib, whose health gradually deteriorated, Jonah kept searching for answers around the palace premises. He wasn't sure how exactly the Prince was being poisoned, but he could feel it in his bones that he was. Desperate for answers, he started learning about slow poisoning and searched for other possible ways that one could be poisoned. He did not come to a conclusion, but he kept his research going.

One day, as Jonah was on one of his morning runs, he saw dark clouds approaching above the courtyard. Normally, he would take this sign of weather as a precaution and return inside, but for some reason, this time, he simply ignored his intuitions and carried on with his run. Sooner rather than later, it started pouring down heavy rain before Jonah reached half the mark of his usual running distance.

Finally listening to what nature had been telling him, Jonah went straight back to the palace, and as soon as he got his foot in the door, the weather turned for the worse, and it started pouring hail.

"The forecast had constantly predicted that it would rain heavily today, sir," Tobias said as he passed behind Jonah in the foyer.

"I suppose we sometimes forget to pay attention to obvious things," Jonah said.

Just then, it was as if a bell went off in Jonah's head, and he was immediately reminded of something that Flagstaff often said. Jonah remembered that he used to say, *"Even though we often forget how to find the focal point, do pay attention to the obvious things."* Jonah felt as if he was missing something crucial in Najib's case. Something that was staring at him in the face but that he simply could not put his finger on.

Jonah thought about all the facts of the case again. The only logical explanation he could come up with for Najib's condition was that he was being poisoned; however, that did not seem likely as others tasted the food before Najib, and they were just fine. Furthermore, various doctors had been brought in to examine Najib, but they could not confirm whether it was so without running proper tests.

Later that night, as Jonah went to have a chat with Najib while taking a cup of tea to his room, he was suddenly struck with an idea. He poured one cup for his friend, one for himself, and then sat in his chair while staring out the window.

"Maybe it is not the food at all," Jonah muttered to himself.

"What?" Najib asked.

"Huh?" Jonah asked in return.

"You said maybe it is not the food at all," Najib said as a perplexed expression formed on his face.

"I do not know what you mean, dear friend," Jonah said calmly.

"Jonah, my stomach has betrayed me, and so has my throat after all the vomiting," Najib murmured, and his voice got coarser as he spoke, *"But my ears are doing fine, my friend. It will be another thing entirely if you do not wish to share what you have been thinking about so intensely ever since dinner last night."*

Jonah contemplated and fiddled with his teacup. He had this odd habit of fiddling with his fingers whenever he had to think hard about what to say or what to do next. This was primarily the reason he had taken up arms as a teenager. His hands had finally known what to do when he got nervous, and slowly but surely, his nerves started to calm down until he became one of the most proficient sharp shooters people had ever come across.

"It's something like that, Najib," Jonah continued as he tried relaxing his nerves. He figured that he simply had to let Najib know the truth. *"You see, I have been making some investigation as to why this has been happening to you."*

"What do you mean?" Najib asked as he set the teacup aside on his side table. *"What sort of investigation are you referring to?"*

"Najib, I believe that this condition of yours is not normal, and I do not think you have some sort of cancer-like symptoms in your family. So, I think you have been poisoned, and I have been trying my best to get a hold of some really good doctors and physicians to come and have a look at you," Jonah continued. *"I know it will not be a good idea to take you to a hospital because if the weather somehow turned even worse, there is no telling what could happen along the way. The car could get stuck; you could catch a cold on top of everything else that you are facing, and not to mention, we could get attacked again."*

"Oh, Jonah. I can see the worry on your face," Najib responded. *"I get where you are coming from, but I do think that this is merely some bad stomach flu from a dish I might have eaten during my trips. Nothing more."*

"But, Najib, you do not understand. This could be something dire!" Jonah uttered. *"You are my family, Najib. The only person left alive that I consider my family. So, it is out of the question that I would not at least try to figure out what is going wrong with your health."*

Najib simply nodded and said, *"Alright, Jonah. If it brings you some satisfaction, and that is what your instincts are telling you, then I trust you. Find out what you can and if you need me to understand something along the way, or if you need help where I do not have to do something excessive, then let me know."*

"Thank you, Najib. I just know that things are happening right in front of our very eyes, and somehow, we are missing it," Jonah replied.

"You mean to say you already have a suspect in mind? This fast?" Najib enquired.

"Not exactly. But I do think that it might be what is keeping you hydrated for a while," Jonah added, stirring the tea in his cup. *"It's the water, Najib. The bottled water that is brought straight into your room, and nobody else drinks from it."*

"That can't be. It's packaged in a factory, Jonah," Najib said as a perplexed look formed on his face.

"I know I do not have my proof yet, but I will soon. By then, I merely ask for your trust, dear friend," Jonah replied. He knew he would have to prove to the Prince that what his intuition was telling him had never been wrong. Not only that, but Jonah had to gather proof before anything worse happened to the Prince's health. Or worse if something irreversible happened. Jonah knew in his heart that he would never be able to forgive himself if he did not at least try to find out what was going on and who was behind it.

Chapter 20: Proof

Jonah got up from his chair and placed the teacup in his hand on the table beside it. He then moved toward the crate of water bottles placed in the Prince's room. Jonah could see clearly that the Prince was brought two to three crates of personalized bottled water at a time. That was because he always chose to keep himself hydrated and stocked up whenever he planned to stay in the palace for a long time.

Jonah picked up a bottle and smelled it. All the while, Najib kept staring at him to get a clue of what he was trying to imply. Then, as if on cue, he said, *"Jonah, you are not trying to say that it is the water I drink every day that has gotten me sick, are you?"*

"Najib, I may be wrong. But right now, this is the only logical explanation to me," Jonah answered. *"I mean, think about it. No one gets to taste it before you do, no one even gets their hands on some of these bottles for themselves, and most importantly, this water getting to you and you drinking it without question is a done deal."*

Jonah started pacing around the room while he smelled the water bottle in his hand to decipher if he could figure out anything from the scent, but as much as he tried, he could not figure out what was in it besides water.

"But, Jonah, don't you think that if there was something in it, I would have tasted it?" Najib asked.

"That is exactly what I thought," Jonah said. *"So, do you mind if I taste the water from this bottle in my hand?"*

"Go ahead," Najib replied and watched Jonah closely.

Jonah brought the bottle to his mouth, and as soon as he was about to take a drink, Najib yelled out, *"Stop, Jonah! I do not know if what you are telling me is the truth or not. But I do not wish to take a chance with it. Honestly, I give you permission to investigate further with any intuition that you might have. The only way to find out if it is true and if this water supply is slowly poisoning me is to take a couple of samples and get them tested."*

"You are right," Jonah replied as he closed the bottle cap and put it in his inside jacket pocket. *"I have a few places in mind where I can go to check this out. Incognito, of course. I do not wish to arouse any suspicion from anyone, and for that reason, I shall be leaving the palace by myself. Frankly, Najib, I do not trust anyone but you at the moment, and I want to keep it that way until my doubts are cleared."*

"Very well," Najib added as Jonah was about to take his leave. *"I will not ask for you to take anyone with you, but perhaps it will be a good idea to disguise yourself as a local. You stand out like a sore thumb during the Egyptian public, and I do not want you to be followed."*

Jonah nodded and said his goodbyes to the Prince. As he made his way down the hallway corridor and into his bedroom, Jonah wore the traditional galabia (a long, loose shirt) that had been placed in his cupboard as per Najib's orders for a traditional festival coming up soon in the city. Everyone at the palace was meant to attend as it was a traditional and festive affair that the Prince had been carrying out all the way from his father and grandfather.

The news had traveled across town that the Prince was sick and that the festival was going to be delayed for a while. Najib did not want this, of course, but considering the danger he was in, it was advised by Jonah and the others that attending or even holding a festival at a time like this was unwise. There was no way Jonah was going to let Najib attend any sort of festivities while he suffered physically due to unknown circumstances.

So, Jonah put on the traditional garments and fixed his sandy brown hair to be neatly tucked underneath the cap included as part of the wardrobe. His beard and mustache had grown significantly during the last few days, and Jonah knew just how to use them to his advantage. Najib had always been the only person who knew the extent of Jonah's expertise in his line of work. The experience was of doing a lot of undercover work.

So, considering the upcoming auction strategy to lure out his enemy, he had arranged to get a self-coloring and disguise kit to use for Jonah's appearance, more specifically, his hair. Jonah took out that kit and colored his beard and mustache, the color almost similar to that of Najib's, which was midnight black. He had experience with blending into places that required a different manner of the population at different turns. Therefore, after he was done, Jonah took one long look in the mirror and made sure that none of his old self was showing.

Furthermore, the other thing he was completely aware of was that no one must see him leave the palace, or else someone from security, or worse, Abdul or Omar could be alerted. So, Jonah made sure while he was staying at the palace that he knew of all available exits from the palace. Therefore, underneath his clothes, Jonah had tied up his bullet vest, gun, extra bullets, and the knives he usually carried. He wore a backpack along with the attire, not only to carry the water bottle samples but also to have room for the reports he would obtain from the laboratories.

Time was of the essence as Jonah rushed from his room after equipping himself with all the necessities and down the stairs. After the coast was clear, he made his way out the back exit through the kitchen and the pantry. He could see Omar and Abdul having a cigarette outside, but it was not long until they were done and proceeded to go toward the car garage where they usually hung out. Omar was a bit of a car fanatic, but Abdul was not.

After Jonah saw them leave, he swiftly but quietly headed outside the door and grabbed one of the Prince's

Mountain bikes parked there. He grabbed the bike that Najib liked to use, as it was the strongest, and he proceeded on his way straight to a laboratory.

As soon as Jonah got inside the laboratory of a huge hospital in the city, he walked into the lobby and thought to mimic Najib's accent as soon as he came up to the lady at the hospital administration desk.

"Hello, madam," Jonah spoke calmly but with a slight worry in his voice. *"I was wondering if you could guide me to the lab to get some tests done?"*

"Oh sure, sir," the administrator replied. *"What sort of test do you want to get done? So that I can guide you to the relevant area."*

"Oh, I actually have a sample here with me, and I was wondering if I could meet with a lab expert in private," Jonah whispered as he took out a police badge that he had stolen from Omar. This one had neither a photo nor badge number, just a gold medallion. *"You see, I am from the police, and I am conducting a secret investigation. So, I would deeply appreciate it if you could take me to the expert without arousing suspicion, of course."*

"Oh my... Oh, I understand," the administrator whispered back. *"Of course, sir, come right this way."*

Thankfully, the lab Jonah entered was empty except for a lean-looking bearded man hunched over a microscope at the far end of the lab. The administrator left and closed the door behind her. Jonah walked up to the man who was presumable a scientist and said, *"Sir, I am sorry to disturb you, but I wonder if you can help me."*

"Who are you?" The man asked as he looked up from the microscope.

"Inspector Mahmoud, I am a police officer, and I need you to run some tests on a couple of samples to tell me what exactly is in it and how harmful it is," Jonah replied calmly and confidently as he pulled out the water bottles from his backpack and stretched out his hand to reveal the police badge.

"Hmm. I was wondering if this was going to be another regular day or if I was finally going to get something interesting to work with," the scientist replied. *"Well, here you are, inspector. Call me Doctor Khaled."*

Dr. Khaled took the bottles in his already glove-covered hands and poured a bit of the water onto a petri dish. *"Grab a mask and gloves from above that counter, inspector. I do not want you to contaminate any of the things here, "* the good doctor said. *"Or vice versa."*

Jonah did as he was told and followed the doctor over to another microscope across the back wall. The man looked through the microscope two separate times as he poured each of the bottles' contents into separate petri dishes. As soon as he had looked through them thoroughly, his face scrunched up in confusion.

"What? What is it, Doctor?" Jonah asked.

"Come here and look," Dr. Khaled answered and moved aside to let Jonah have a look.

"What exactly am I looking at, Doctor?" Jonah asked without removing his face from the viewer of the microscope.

"You see those tiny yellow specs among the water?" the doctor said. *"That is carbon monoxide, inspector."*

"What does it do?" Jonah asked. His curiosity was piqued.

"Carbon monoxide is otherwise known as the Invisible Killer for human beings," the doctor continued. *"It is a colorless, odorless, poisonous gas."*

The doctor then carried on explaining just how much damage it could do if human beings were exposed to it in small doses. Jonah had told the doctor that the case he was investigating was where a victim had been poisoned by it. So, the doctor went on to explain that exposure to carbon monoxide could cause flu-like symptoms that could be fatal.

"Doctor, tell me the symptoms of this poisoning, please. Like what we should watch out for," Jonah asked him.

"CO poisoning victims may initially suffer symptoms like nausea, fatigue, headaches, dizziness, confusion, and breathing difficulty," Dr. Khaled told him. *"Moreover, when victims inhale CO, or in this case, ingest it through water, the toxic gas enters the bloodstream and causes vomiting along with nausea and fatigue."*

"So, is there a chance to save the person?" Jonah asked. *"Or is death the only option? Because judging by what you are telling me, Doc, the person can die quickly from it."*

"Inspector, the cure does exist," the doctor replied. *"Although I shall have to see the victim first in order to administer it myself. The cure is called hyperbaric oxygen therapy. It involves breathing pure oxygen in a chamber where the air pressure is about two to three times higher than normal. Now, how it helps is that it speeds up the replacement of carbon monoxide with oxygen in your blood. Thus, curing the patient slowly but effectively."*

A kind of relief crept over Jonah's face, and he visibly sighed and said, *"Thank you, doctor. You have no idea how much this has helped. I shall see you shortly with the patient."*

With that said, Jonah left the lab and rushed straight back to the palace with the lab reports hidden deep within his backpack, along with the lab doctor's number. Since it was now confirmed that the Prince was being slowly poisoned, Jonah had proof of it all to present to him. All he needed to do now was make sure Najib was well and recovered.

Chapter 21: Private Investigation

Jonah arrived back at the palace on the trusty mountain bike he had borrowed from the Prince's garage near the kitchen pantry. His mind was racing from everything that Doctor Khaled had told him about the Carbon Monoxide poisoning and how the victim suffering from it could be in severe and irreversible danger when they encountered it. Therefore, Jonah knew exactly what he needed to do to get Najib back into shape.

After arriving back at the palace, Jonah made his way straight to his bedroom and changed into his regular clothes. He took the documents out of his backpack and read them closely as to what the results said precisely. Judging by the quantity of poison in those bottles, Jonah had no choice but to change the Prince's water supply first. He rushed to see Najib, and as soon as he made eye contact with him, Jonah could see clearly that the condition of Najib's health had further deteriorated in the short while that he was gone.

Najib's skin looked sickly pale, and he had huge bags under his eyes. He had also lost quite a bit of weight in the last few weeks. He could not speak clearly as the poison had gotten into his lungs. There was no way that he would last any longer if his water supply was not changed. Jonah could not bear to see his best friend in this condition any longer, so he decided that in order to speed up the process, he needed one other person's help.

Jonah went straight to the phone on the Prince's bedside table and rang the kitchen, where Tobias usually would be throughout the day. *"Yes, Tobias, this is Jonah,"* he spoke.

"Yes, sir. What can I help you with?" Tobias replied.

"I was wondering if you could send Abdul to the Prince's room?" Jonah continued. *"There is something that the Prince and I would like to speak to him about."*

"Certainly," Tobias answered.

The entire time, Najib kept watching closely and had this knowing look on his face that there was something up Jonah's sleeve. The Prince was completely aware that Jonah knew what he was doing, and if anything, he would put Najib's health as the first priority.

"Najib, I need you to listen to me. When Abdul comes in here, I need you to back me," Jonah whispered to Najib as he put down the receiver. *"There is something important I have discovered, and what I will tell you, for now, is that I was right. You are being poisoned through your water intake, and somehow, they have gotten a hold of one of the most lethal poisons known to the human body."*

Najib merely nodded in agreement as he was currently in no position to talk.

"By tonight, I shall arrange with Tobias to get a respirator and oxygen treatment fitted into your bedroom, and not only that, but I have found a brilliant doctor who will cure this poisoning within your system," Jonah added. *"What I need right now is Abdul's help in figuring out how this poison was made to find you directly."*

Najib closed his eyes and merely nodded again. There was a knock at the door, and Abdul entered Najib's room. He stood next to Jonah at the end of the Prince's bed.

"I was told that I was needed here, my Prince," Abdul said to Najib. *"How may I help?"*

"Abdul, there is something I must tell you, but before I reveal it, I must have your word that no one else in the palace will be privy to this conversation," Jonah said as he took a seat next to Najib's bed.

Abdul looked to Jonah and then back to Najib, almost as a way of getting approval from his Prince and that whatever he was about to agree to was being backed by his Prince before anyone else. Najib agreed by nodding *yes* and then looked toward Jonah and tilted his head in a manner that said, *"Carry on."*

"Abdul, I had a suspicion that the Prince was being poisoned, but I couldn't seem to figure out how since

everything that comes through the kitchen is first tasted by you and Tobias. But then it struck me; maybe it didn't come from the kitchen after all," Jonah explained and then pointed toward the water bottles placed on Najib's dresser.

"I had a sneaking suspicion that perhaps his water supply had been poisoned since that is the only thing that the Prince consumes directly without anyone's involvement," Jonah said. He then took out the lab reports from the inside pocket of his jacket.

"This morning, I snuck out to conduct my own investigation based on a simple hunch. I want to say that this was only because I did not wish to arouse any suspicion among the castle staff. After all, frankly, I do not trust anyone other than the Prince at the moment. Please do not take this the wrong way because I know how much experience you and Omar have when it comes to protecting Najib," Jonah said.

Jonah handed over the lab reports to Abdul for a read and waited for him to look over the facts for himself. Abdul did so, and his eyes displayed shock and anger in equal measure.

"Tell me then something, Jonah," Abdul said as he returned the reports to Jonah. *"Why have you decided now that you would like my assistance if it is true that you do not trust anyone here?"* he asked.

"Because I believe that we need to find the culprit here as soon as possible before they find out any other means to harm Najib," Jonah answered. *"We might not be as quick next time, so we better be two steps ahead in this moment. I also want to find out where it is that this culprit got a hold of Najib's private water supply and how did they know that only Najib was the one who drank it? Only someone on the inside would be privy to that investigation, which makes me think that we have a rat in our midst,"* Jonah said.

Abdul looked to Najib for reassurance, and he nodded in agreement. This was the only signal Abdul needed because his face showed instant determination. Even if there was a slight chance that Jonah's suspicions were true and that not even Omar and Abdul could be trusted, he still had to give that man a chance to help him save the Prince. So, this was Jonah's chance to see for himself if the dedication was indeed there and that Abdul would not use this chance to accelerate Najib's downfall by any means necessary.

"My Prince," Abdul bowed to Najib and said, *"I will not let you down, and Mr. Jonah, I am honored that you have trusted me with this information, as I know how dear you are to my Prince. To be honest, I had been worried for the past few days with confusion as to what had suddenly happened. But I now know that my duties are needed here before any such answer can be found."*

Chapter 22: Catching the Culprit

"We are grateful to you, Abdul," Jonah replied after Abdul agreed to help them catch the culprit. "And Najib, please hold yourself from drinking any water from there until we get back."

Then, as if struck with a new idea, Jonah said, "Wait a second." He rushed out of the bedroom and instantly returned with a freshly made jug of citrus water from his own bedroom and placed it right beside Najib on his side table. He poured a glass from that jug and gave it to Najib. The Prince drank it and displayed a new sense of relief. Even though the water jug was simply regular water, the men in that room needed to see that they could not only trust one another in this matter but also keep Najib safe before they had a chance to uncover the truth on their own terms.

Najib nodded again slightly and then tilted his head toward the door. This was his way of telling the two men to get on with their mission. So, by the time Abdul and Jonah left Najib's room, night had fallen already, and every single servant had gone to bed. The only person they could hear making a little bit of noise was Tobias in the kitchen. He was also just leaving when Jonah and Abdul entered the kitchen.

"What are you two gentlemen doing here at this hour? Is there something I can help you with? Or should I fetch the cook to make you something to eat if you are hungry?"

"That won't be necessary, Tobias. Najib has run out of water, so we came to fetch him some bottles. Can you please show us where his water supply is stored?" Jonah asked.

Tobias looked curiously between Jonah and Abdul.

"Sir, you did not have to come all the way here. I would have brought them to the Prince myself," Tobias said.

"It is fine, Tobias. Now that we are here, we might as well bring them back," Jonah said.

"Very well, sir. Follow me," Tobias said as he led the two men to the back of the kitchen and toward the storage area.

"Thank you, Tobias. We'll find our way out," Jonah told him.

Taking that as his cue, Tobias left the two men in the storage room.

Before heading to the kitchen, Abdul and Jonah had planned what they would do in Najib's room. They planned to hold a small stakeout in the storage room where Najib's water supply was stored.

After Tobias left the two, they hid behind boxes of food stored in the corner, giving them a clear view of the crates of water bottles. Now all that was left to do was to wait and see if someone came to ruffle the water supply of their Prince.

Jonah and Abdul waited for what felt like an eternity for someone to enter the storage room. Since they had hidden quite well behind the storage boxes, they had a clear view of whoever would enter from the storage room's back entrance. Both Abdul and Jonah were aware of the fact that Tobias had a habit of locking up each door of the palace and double-checking them before he went to bed. So, if someone were to enter, they would have to be an expert at picking locks.

"It is almost midnight. How long do you think before the culprit comes?" Abdul asked Jonah as they had been sitting in the storage room for a couple of hours now.

"I am not sure, to be honest," Jonah answered. "It could take the entire night, but on the other hand, it may only take a few minutes. Depends on the range of the operation, I think. But here, I do not think we would have to wait much longer," Jonah said, his eyes never leaving the back entrance.

"Why do you think that?" Abdul questioned.

"Because I feel like this deed is being done by just one person," Jonah replied. "I think that this requires a level of mystique that only one man can do at a time. If there were more than one person, we would have had some clue as to who they could be or even how many they could be," Jonah replied.

"That is true," Abdul agreed.

As the watch on Jonah's wrist struck midnight, the slow clicking of the door lock alerted both Jonah's and Abdul's ears. Someone was attempting a break-in. The lock was opened, and shortly afterward, the sound of footsteps lightly grazed their ears, making Abdul and Jonah go into their defense mode. Something they both noticed was that the man walked in a certain delicate manner that confused the two.

A figure came into view, covered in black from head to toe, with the hood of their jacket completely covering their face. Not only that, but the two men saw that the culprit was also wearing a mask to cover their face and gloves to cover their hands. However, despite the jacket, the silhouette of the figure and the way they moved had given them away. It was a woman.

She walked with the silence of a cat and came near the crates. She put their hands in her jacket and pulled something out. Jonah could make out that it was a syringe. Then, she swiftly started injecting something into the water bottles in the crate that was aptly labeled "For the Prince." It's safe to say that she was very agile in her approach. Abdul and Jonah wasted no time because they now had enough proof to take action.

As soon as they saw they had a clear shot of the culprit, they both tackled her to the ground. Jonah held the woman down with both hands while Abdul rushed to turn all the lights on inside the storage room to see who their mystery criminal was. After the lights turned on, Jonah ripped the mask from the woman's face to reveal someone that he could not have predicted to be involved in this, even in his wildest dreams. He was absolutely blown away to find Nadia on the ground.

"Oh my God...." Jonah muttered under his breath. Those were the only words he could muster after the shock he felt from tackling Nadia as she was busy injecting poison into Najib's water supply. His hands shook as he held Nadia to the ground.

"Jonah, get up. We must cuff her!" Abdul yelled over Jonah to bring him back from his shock, which actually worked. In a spell of a second, the confusion and shock Jonah had on his face were replaced by anger and hurt. But more so, just rage. Jonah felt this burning anger coursing through his body, and he stood up and picked up Nadia with him.

"The rage I feel for you is actually forcing me not to kill you right this second, Nadia," Jonah whispered under grinding teeth. "Because as much as I would like to, you are not my culprit to deal with. It will be Najib who will figure out what to do with you. But mark my words, woman, whatever he decides, I will back him a hundred percent."

Nadia stayed quiet but scowled as she rolled her eyes at Jonah. Not only did her body language express that she did not care that it was Jonah who had found her, but she also did not give a damn about what she was caught doing. It was almost as if she was just waiting for someone to discover her.

Meanwhile, Abdul had proceeded to label the injected batch as one that would be thrown out and not given to the Prince. He then joined Jonah and handcuffed Nadia to take her in front of the Prince.

Once they reached Najib's door, Jonah suddenly came to a halt.

"What? What is it?" Abdul asked Jonah.

"I have arranged for a doctor to come and see Najib first thing in the morning, and he is sleeping right now after taking his medication," Jonah replied calmly as he realized that the first priority he had was having Najib be in better health to deal with Nadia. "I think we should lock her up till morning and deal with her when Najib has been given the oxygen treatment to heal for a little while. Maybe in that state, he will fully be able to know what to do about Nadia."

Abdul nodded as he could see why Jonah had this realization. There was absolutely no way that Nadia's judgment was going to weigh more than the Prince's health. So, Abdul took Nadia, already handcuffed, down to the basement, where Najib had a few holding cells built for when his enemies got braver than they predicted. Abdul searched every pocket of Nadia's outfit and then left her in a holding cell, planning to come get her and present her in front of the Prince in the morning after the doctor's visit. The cell was locked twice afterward, and so was the corridor that led up to the cells. Abdul knew what he was doing as he had led the building of those cells in the first place.

In the meantime, Jonah went back to his room and paced around his bedroom, wracking his brain, trying to figure out why Nadia would do something like that. All he knew was that Najib had introduced Jonah to her and said they could very well hit it off if they wished to be acquainted as more than friends. Moreover, Nadia had agreed, so no matter how hard Jonah tried to figure out the reasons, he could not understand what Nadia's reasoning behind it all was.

Chapter 23: Punishment

The morning arrived and Jonah had already woken up before anyone else to welcome Doctor Khaled to run some tests on Najib and get him on the oxygen treatment he had told Jonah about. Soon, the good doctor arrived at the palace and brought a couple of his assistants with him to help Najib. The assistants had been thorough from the beginning of the treatment to the end, and Jonah stayed by Najib's side throughout.

Jonah knew that as soon as the Prince was in a good enough condition to talk after the treatment and had attained a reasonable amount of rest from it, he would bring Nadia forward to meet with Najib. This would not only give Najib a chance to meet the culprit responsible for his failing health but also give her the sentence she deserved. The more Jonah thought about why Nadia did what she did, the more she slipped away from his heart. Initially, he had been very shocked and genuinely hurt, but now, whatever feelings he had for her were slowly but surely fading away.

There was one thing that Jonah could never bring himself to forgive someone for, and that was deception. Nadia had proven from her actions that her hatred toward Najib must have been so deep that it disregarded everything he and Nadia had faced together. At least, that is what Jonah figured. But whatever the truth was, Jonah would wait until she faced Najib to uncover it once and for all.

Najib woke up after two hours of the treatment. Still groggy from having his mouth covered with the oxygen mask, he tried speaking, but merely a whisper came out. Jonah had been standing near the window, looking out onto the flowers in the courtyard, when he heard a sudden movement coming from Najib's direction. He turned around and rushed to his best friend's side to see that he was finally awake.

"Shh, do not try to talk just yet, my friend," Jonah spoke calmly, yet the joy in his voice was quite evident. "*I am so glad that you are awake, Najib. How do you feel? You can just blink once if you feel better than yesterday.*"

Najib smiled and spoke in a whispered tone, *"I am so much better, thanks to you, my dearest friend."*

Jonah felt the emotions running through him. He felt as though he had almost lost his best friend, who was not just a friend but a brother. *"I am just relieved, believe me,"* Jonah said as he wiped a tear from his eye. *"I do have something to tell you, though, and it is rather urgent,"* Jonah continued, his expression changing.

"What is it?" Najib asked.

"Abdul and I have discovered who it is that is responsible for this happening to you," Jonah said as he gestured to Najib and the oxygen cylinder standing beside Najib's bed.

The shocked expression on Najib's face and the fact that he was speechless after what Jonah had said was a clear indication to Jonah of what he wanted to know. *"My friend, I not only wish to tell you who it is, but I can do better. I will show you,"* Jonah said as he got up from his seat beside Najib's bed. *"Hold that thought, and I will be right back."*

Jonah rushed out of Najib's room and found Abdul sipping a cup of tea with Tobias and Omar in the palace kitchen. He quickly told them all that the Prince was awake, and he was able to speak, albeit in a whispered tone. After sharing a knowing look with each other, it was like all 'hands on deck!' Abdul ran down to the basement and brought Nadia upstairs in handcuffs in case she tried to do anything smart.

Nadia was brought into Najib's room, and the Prince was stunned, to say the least. Najib lifted his arm and beckoned silently to Jonah to help him sit up in his bed. Jonah quickly obliged, and Najib tilted his head in confusion as to why Nadia had been brought in. Surely, he thought that this was some sort of sick joke. But before Najib could clear his denial and ask why Nadia was suddenly standing in his room in handcuffs, she broke down in front of him and sank to the floor.

"Najib, I did it all to avenge myself! You have to understand!" Nadia yelled. *"You have no idea how it feels like to have been wronged by you!"*

"What the hell do you mean, Nadia?" Jonah chimed in. In contrast, Najib sat silently as he gave Nadia the most lethal death stare that made even Omar and Abdul silent. But since Jonah was not looking in Najib's direction, he asked Nadia to explain herself clearly. *"Well, go on and tell us, woman. What is the meaning of this?!"*

"Oh, I will tell you," Nadia yelled through tears as she pointed toward the Prince. *"That man not only took my youth away but also refused to accept me as one of his brides. Oh, and he knows that he was quite capable of taking me as his wife, but he did not! He refused to marry me after he came on to me all those years ago."*

Najib had enough of Nadia's whining and spoke up. *"We were young, and do not forget, Nadia, I was hesitant about you from the start. It was you who ran away from your home and snuck into my hotel room that night. So, to tell you the truth, my gut instincts have never led me astray. I was always hesitant about keeping you in my life, and I had told you that from the beginning. But when you appeared that day and Jonah was so taken with you after he saw you, I decided not to say anything."*

Jonah sat in his chair after this series of shocking revelations. His face half covered by his hands, Jonah remained completely silent as he looked between Najib and Nadia. All that was running through his mind was why Najib would keep this from him for so long. Nadia could not reply after Najib's statements and simply stood up and looked at him in anger.

"Ever since I saw how you and Jonah got along, I thought, 'Finally, she will now have someone with whom she can form a bond with and forget about the past.' But I was so sadly mistaken, Nadia. Wasn't I? If I had known your intentions were this vile, I would have never crossed paths with you at all," Najib spoke in a tone that was resolute of the fact that he had already made the decision in his mind on what he was about to say next. The Prince took a pause and then looked toward Jonah and asked, *"Do you trust my decisions, Jonah?"*

Jonah sat up straight in his chair and looked at Najib, completely resolved about the fact that he was thinking the same thing his friend was about to do and say.

"Of course, I do, Najib," Jonah replied.

"Omar, Abdul," Najib beckoned in their direction.

"Yes, my Prince," they answered instantly.

"Make sure she does not see the light of day again," Najib said in the coldest tone possible. *"Since she decided that she wanted to take the air away from my lungs, I want this to be the last time this woman breathes."*

"As you wish, my Prince," Abdul agreed, while Omar simply nodded. They both grabbed Nadia by an arm and

took her out of Najib's room as she screamed and yelled profanities at Najib and Jonah.

In the meantime, Jonah simply closed his eyes, buried his head in his hands, and said, *"To think I actually liked her at one point in my life."*

"I know, my friend," Najib added. *"But I hope we can heal from this."*

"I hope so too," Jonah replied, but he still could not shake a sinking feeling that sparked within him as soon as Nadia was taken out of the room. Jonah was keeping suspicions that it ended too easily. He kept thinking that maybe there was more to her story than she led everyone else to believe.

Chapter 24: The Infamous Cousin

Knock Knock

Jonah's bedroom door was knocked about half a dozen times by now, but he was still in dreamland, dozed off in his bed. It had been a long time since the palace had known any semblance of peace. Nadia was taken care of a couple of days ago, and Najib was doing much better after taking oxygen treatment constantly for the last few days. The way things were going, the only thing left to do was take the final mission head-on and charge the enemy with all they had.

Jonah finally jolted awake because of the incessant rapping on his door and yelled, "Alright, all right... I'm coming! Jeez, what is with you guys?!" He lazily pulled his feet off the bed and went straight to open the door, but he could not have expected or known who was behind it. To his surprise, it was Najib himself. While Najib had been getting the treatment, he was still advised bed rest by the doctor, so Jonah was surprised but also elated at the same time to see his dear friend out and about.

"Najib? Oh my God! I am so glad to see you out of bed in the morning! How are you feeling? Do your lungs still hurt? Come inside and sit down, won't you!?" Jonah exclaimed. He was genuinely glad that his friend was recovering.

Najib laughed heartily and hugged Jonah as he came inside the room. "Slow down, my friend!" Najib replied in a calm but still rather hoarse voice. "I am doing pretty well, actually. My heart rate is good, and I went for a walk this morning. But, before I get into how I was doing this morning in great detail, I want to tell you that this entire experience has shown me who I want to declare as my family. Jonah, you have shown a great deal of resilience and love when it came to a decision about what was going on with my health," Najib said.

"Why do you have to thank me, Najib?" Jonah questioned. "You know that you would have done the same thing if the shoe was on the other foot. At this point in our lives, and considering how much distress we have seen together, I can safely say that I trust you with my life. So, that is why I did not think twice when I wanted to investigate all that was going on with you."

"I agree with you," Najib said as he caught a few tears trickling down his cheeks. "Jonah, my family has given me all they could, and the ones that genuinely cared about me have left this Earth. That is why I have always been fearful of the love I sometimes receive from others, thinking that it might not be genuine and that they must have some ulterior motive to get to some of my prized possessions. But ever since you have shown me how much of a brother you truly are to me, even if we have opposite backgrounds, I don't know what to gift you in return. Except for the fact that you are now entitled to share what God and good fortune has blessed me with."

"You do not have to do that, Najib," Jonah replied. "But what we can do now is get back to what we were initially planning to do. That is to get vengeance in the best way possible. The only way we know how."

With that said, they both knew instantly that the only way things would go back to the way they were was if they got back to focusing on their mission.

With Najib now recovering, the auction was set a few days from that day. So, they set about planning everything down to the most miniature details.

Najib knew that his mission was not complete as they still had to take down Najib's cousin to ensure his safety, and it made him uneasy. The day arrived, and they all assembled in the palace's arsenal room, which was situated just near the shooting range near the back. Abdul and Omar equipped themselves with the most state-of-the-art weaponry that Najib had gathered over the years, as he knew that someday he would need to use it. They got ready to execute the plan, but all the while, Jonah had this sinking feeling that things might not go as smoothly as they would like to.

Nevertheless, Jonah and the others readied themselves for the showdown of their lives while being equipped with their choice of weapons. Abdul and Omar were brilliant sharpshooters and snipers, so they equipped themselves with one close-range weapon each and strapped a lightweight sniper rifle on their backs. By the looks of those guns, they would be heavy to carry for anyone of average height and weight, but since Abdul and Omar were both burly, it looked easy as pie.

All the while, Jonah tried to push his intuitive senses aside that it all was going a little too smoothly. They all reached the venue and disguised themselves according to plan. Omar and Abdul had known from way before the plan even began what they needed to do, and they did exactly that. Both took their place outside the venue, where they would see first-hand how many guards would arrive with Najib's cousin, Habib.

It was a well-known fact that Habib had at least three men to always guard him. However, since this auction had been advertised as a low-key and high-profile auction with zero publicity, he had only brought those three men and no one else. Jonah used the disguise kit as authentically as possible, as he did during the time, he had planned to pay a visit to the local lab in order to get the sample water tested.

As planned, Jonah functioned as the auctioneer as he had always done and not only guarded the diamond on stage as it was displayed but also hid his firearms quite well so that nobody could see them. As soon as Jonah brought the pink diamond on stage, it instantly captured everyone in the audience's attention. Placed safely in a bullet-proof glass cage, the diamond was safe and secure. But still, Jonah kept his hands sneakily on his strapped gun to make sure that he would catch even the slightest of tricky movements.

The people from the previous auctions had gotten a taste of what he was capable of on stage, so he masked his voice quite well too. He did not feel the need to take out any of his firearms until they all saw Najib's cousin, Habib, enter the venue. The man was dressed in bold colors from head to toe, and it was in a way that anyone passing by would not put him under the category of 'regular.' Moreover, there would always be a chance that someone ever trying to cross that man's path would get insulted for simply breathing the same air.

Habib took his place at the front of the venue while his guards stayed outside. At the same time, Jonah pulled on his shirt collar to activate the signal to Najib that his cousin was there. Najib was, otherwise, cleverly hidden behind the stage door with a silenced revolver in hand to take the money shot. Najib wanted to be the one to shoot his cousin as he simply did not want the blood of his enemy on anyone else's hands.

Just then, Najib's earpiece buzzed; Omar informed him that Habib's guards had been taken care of outside. The few guards that Najib's cousin had brought with him were easily taken out by those two. They had proven to be relatively weak compared to the brute strength of Omar and Abdul.

Najib stood up from behind the stage and, for a split second, locked eyes with his cousin. Habib was shell-shocked as soon as he saw his cousin face to face, even if it was from a great distance. Najib took the chance and did not hesitate, and the bullet from his gun went straight between Habib's eyebrows. A single shot from his weapon took out the enemy he had been wronged by for so long. The folks sitting in the seats around him screamed as Najib's cousin slumped over in his chair. Meanwhile, Jonah made sure that he yelled out to each and every member of the auction to leave the venue.

"All of you are not in any danger. The person who was the target of this auction is now dead. You can all go home now," Jonah beckoned over the microphone.

As everyone slowly cleared out from the venue, Omar and Abdul grabbed the body and wrapped it in parachute-like fabric tightly. They dumped it in the back of the security vehicle and let Najib know they were ready to leave. Najib followed them and sat in his own car with Jonah. The team had altogether decided that they would dump the body in the deepest chasm of a cave that was just outside of the desert area.

The four men took the body to the cave and burned it before any tourists would be able to take a chance and visit the area. After seeing a solemn expression on Jonah's face, Najib asked, "You okay, my friend?"

"Oh yes, I am doing fine. It's just a little squirmy feeling in my gut. I am sure it's nothing," Jonah replied.

Everything had gone according to plan, and while Najib celebrated the death of his biggest enemy at the end of the day, Jonah could not help but have the same detached feeling as if all of this was too good to be true.

Chapter 25: Too Good to Be True

Jonah, as usual, stood in the background while Abdul and Omar packed their arsenal into the back of their truck. Jonah wanted to observe if there was any more danger looming; he always had two armed bodyguards standing. He had a habit of sticking around a location after a mission was completed just to see if there was something that they missed or someone who had been waiting for the mission to go just as easily as it had that day.

If there was one feeling that Jonah just could not shake, it was that, considering the previous auction, this one had gone particularly smoothly. So, he thought it would not hurt to go back to the venue and check it out, just in case.

"You guys, go ahead and go back to the palace. I think I have to check the venue before we can be absolutely sure that this was indeed as easy as it seems," Jonah said as he put a new case of extra bullets into his holster next to the gun strapped to his ribcage.

"What do you mean? It's not safe for you alone, Jonah," Najib replied and got out of the passenger door in the front.

"This is something that I need to do, Najib. Otherwise, I will have this nagging feeling at the back of my head," Jonah added.

"Hmmph. Fine, I cannot do anything about you and your nagging feelings when you get like this," Najib sighed, then added, *"But still, I want Omar to stay with you. That way, I can be certain of your safety and that whatever happens, Omar will be able to report it to me. Is that okay with you?"*

"Of course," Jonah replied. *"Now go before I have to worry about you too."*

They said their goodbyes and kept a couple of weapons each to stay back. Omar gave his brother a half-hearted hug and bid farewell to his Prince. Jonah hugged Najib and told him that both men would be back at the palace in no time to discuss his retirement plan.

***

As Jonah entered the venue, he and Omar saw a door at the corner of the corridor close.

"Omar, I want you to stay here and make sure that whoever comes back out here, you catch them," Jonah whispered to Omar as he grabbed his arm to stop him from lunging at whoever was hiding in the back. Omar agreed and stepped back while Jonah tip-toed around the hall and sneaked toward the corridor. Jonah heard footsteps creeping outside the corridor and into the back lawn of the venue.

In the corner, there stood a strange young woman wearing a large black sun hat and non-descript clothing. He watched her as she kept looking around the lawn as if she was either waiting for someone or watching out for herself. Her hand stayed in her purse as if she was gripping something. This was very unsettling for Jonah. He could not figure out who this woman was and who she could be waiting for while sneakily leading him down the venue.

Jonah did not know what to make of her. This woman's legs looked like they did not know when to quit. She wore high heels that complimented her posture in just the right way. He found her to be attractive, and he certainly wanted to meet her, but he was fearful that she was just another person, and it was too early for this when he was looking for some indication that their mission had gone too easy for a change.

The woman walked slowly, as she must have been aware by now that there was a man following her. Jonah had heard that women could often act on their sixth sense quite quickly. Jonah finally approached her and sat down in the chair beside her. Upon getting closer, Jonah could see that it was indeed a gun she was holding onto. She clutched and held her 0.25 caliber automatic that was in her small purse. She did not know Jonah and thought that he might be a danger to her, but she was just as curious as Jonah was because neither of them was on edge.

"Hi," Jonah said. *"Who are you? And may I ask, why are you here all by yourself? I am assuming that you were here for the auction, but since it ended a while ago, it's strange to be here by yourself, especially after how it ended."*

Her response was short. Avoiding the question, she said, *"Nice shirt, I like it."* It was evident that she was trying to change the subject.

"Alright, let's cut to the chase," Jonah turned to face her and held out his hand to shake hers. *"The name's Jonah. What's yours?"*

"Nevada." She held out her hand fitted in a black silk glove. A gorgeous emerald ring adorned her middle finger, and it looked like it must be worth a fortune. This indicated that she was maybe not there to steal something. But even that was too early to tell. Many jewel thieves wore high-end pieces to mask themselves. *"I know who you are, Mr. Jonah. The famous auctioneer."*

"I guess you do know me," Jonah replied. *"So now that we have got the introductions covered, tell me, is there anything I can do for you? I can drop you home?"* Jonah asked.

"Umm, nothing for now," she responded. *"But maybe we will meet again soon."*

"I'm okay with that," Jonah replied.

*Bang! Bang! *

Suddenly, two loud bangs were heard from the corridor behind them, and with instinct, Jonah lunged at Nevada, hitting the grass, and covering her body, thinking that this was a gunshot aimed at him. Instinctively, he reached inside Nevada's purse that she was holding, touching the cold steel of her revolver. He took it out and pointed it directly at her temple. *"Who hired you?"* Jonah asked. *"Who hired you to kill me?"*

Nevada looked scared and yelled, *"Calm down, Jonah! Don't shoot! No one hired me! I came here to hide and try to get away. Long story short, they are out to kill me. There are people out to kill me, and this was the only place I could think to hide in,"* she said nervously.

Jonah had a bewildered look on his face, a response which meant that he was still not convinced that Nevada was simply not some assassin sent to kill Jonah. He knew that the culprit behind the attacks on Najib was already dead, but he could not help but shake this feeling that Nevada was up to no good. However, the attraction he felt for that woman was almost magnetic, which was understandable because the woman was gorgeous. She was a brunette with strikingly beautiful legs and hazel-brown eyes. This was Jonah's type, to a tee.

Jonah rose from the floor, dusted himself off, and held out his hand to Nevada. If anything, Jonah was not about to forget his Southern roots, even if he was still suspicious of this woman.

"Well, I gotta go now," Nevada said as she straightened her dress. *"Hope to see you soon."*

Jonah replied, "*Sure. That would be nice.*"

Nevada proceeded to go toward the venue exit when she suddenly turned around and said, "*On second thought, I think I will just wait here for a few more minutes. I cannot tell you why because I can see the inquisitive look on your face. But I can say that I just want to leave here safe. That is all.*"

"*Sure,*" Jonah replied and raised both his hands. "*I will not judge or ask any more questions. In fact, I can stay here with you if you'd like?*"

Nevada went quiet for a split second as if she wanted Jonah to be there and leave her alone at the same time. The worry on her face grew slightly and mixed with contemplation, which made Jonah approach her closer and ask, "*You look worried, Nevada. Maybe you could come along with me if that is acceptable to you.*"

Somehow feeling relaxed after a few moments, Nevada replied, "*Okay, yes.*" Jonah asked her to follow him and instructed, "*Stay close.*" They made their way to the rear of the room where Omar was waiting to escort Jonah back to the palace. He sat up and, upon seeing this strange woman accompanying Jonah, he asked, "*Who is this?*"

"*This is Nevada, and she needs our help at the moment,*" Jonah replied. "*Trust me. She will be questioned extensively before even coming near Najib. But I am sure of one thing. She needs to come with us either way.*"

"Okay, if you say so," Omar agreed and revved up the Jeep.

"Jump in," Jonah told her, which she did so quickly. *"Oh, but I forgot. Can I drop you off somewhere? Or I could take you to my home if that is what you prefer?"* Jonah asked.

"Just wherever you are going," Nevada replied. *"I have no baggage, just this duffle bag. I am sorry to keep saying this, but I have to get out of here."*

"I understand," Jonah added. *"I am headed to a friend's place first to pick up my stuff, but then I am on my way to the airport."*

"Okay," Nevada answered as she looked Jonah square in the eyes for the first time. She stared as she had just noticed how much Jonah's eyes reminded her of the ocean. She yearned to be by the sea because, long story short, she was separated from it a long time ago. She wanted to be near it as it simply reminded her of home.

"Nevada, I do not know you," Jonah came up close to her and looked her straight in her eyes before proceeding, *"but for some reason, I want to know you. For that to happen, I will need to watch you and trust that you will not do something dangerous to me. Like, say, murder me when I am not looking because I found you in the place where everyone had left from."*

"I understand that," Nevada replied as she maintained eye contact with Jonah for a second and then looked down.

"I am headed out of the country after I grab my things and say goodbye to my friends," Jonah said. *"It is going to be a private location, but I somehow want to take you with me to find out what your deal is. So, tell me, Nevada, do you want to come with me?"*

Nevada thought, for a few moments, about the people that wanted her dead and replied, *"Sure, yes, that would be terrific. Really, I do not care where it is, but if it will get me out of here, then sure."*

Chapter 26: Goodbyes

Omar drove as Jonah sat in the front seat next to him and Nevada sat in the back, clutching her purse. If Jonah did not trust her, then it was also quite apparent that she did not trust Jonah and Omar either. So, the ride back to the palace was mostly quiet, other than the occasional, 'how long till we get there?' from Nevada, and then 'holy shit!' after she saw that Jonah and Omar had pulled up to a huge mansion.

It took about an hour, but they reached Najib safely, and as Omar went inside, Jonah stayed behind to tell Nevada, *"Wait here by the car. I will get my friend and figure out how we are going to travel together."*

Nevada nodded and leaned against the car.

Jonah came inside and found Najib sitting in the living room with his face buried in the morning newspaper. He rose from the couch and gave Jonah a hug. *"Oh, my friend, I am so glad you are back,"* Najib exclaimed. *"Tobias, fix us a lovely pot of tea, will you? We have a lot to talk about."*

"That we do, my friend," Jonah replied as he and Najib both took a seat on the couch. *"I do have something I would like to speak to you about, Najib. Or better yet, there is someone I want you to meet."*

"Okay...." Najib looked bewildered. But then, he asked with a panicked expression, *"Oh God, please tell me that your suspicions were not proven true? Tell me you did not find another member of my cousin's entourage there at the venue?"*

"No, Najib. Not exactly," Jonah answered. *"Although I did find a woman hiding at the venue. She told me that she was on the run from someone. I have brought her here, and she is outside near the garage. I told her that I am willing to take her with me where I plan to retire to."*

"I see," Najib replied, sighed, and then took a pause. *"How can you trust that she is telling the truth, Jonah? How can you be sure that she is not just some assassin that is sent to kill you?"*

"Honestly, I do not trust her completely," Jonah added. *"That is why I have not invited her inside. But somehow, I believe that she is indeed running from something, and I want to find out what that is."*

"Hmm... If you are certain... then I suppose it will not hurt us to have you try out your suspicions on this very intriguing woman." Najib sighed and then continued, "As you know, your retirement spot has already been chosen, and although I wish that I could keep you here with me forever, I understand that your heart belongs to your hometown and that you yearn for it."

"I know, my friend," Jonah said. *"If you look through the window, you might be able to see her also I do not trust her*

enough to have you go near her after what happened with Nadia. Call it paranoia or whatever."

"Oh, nonsense. I can say hello at a distance, at least," Najib rebutted.

"Well, okay then," Jonah said with a smile as he rose from the sofa, and so did Najib. "I suppose this is goodbye, my friend."

"Not goodbye. This is, until we meet again," Najib said. "You know I will simply be a call away if you need me, my friend?"

"Of course," Jonah replied. "Same goes for you."

Jonah walked up to Omar and Abdul, who had been drinking their tea across the coffee table and hugged them goodbye. "Well, it's been an adventure. And thank you for the hospitality, Tobias." Jonah turned and yelled to the kitchen, to which Tobias simply bowed.

Najib and Jonah walked to the courtyard, and as Najib saw Nevada, he made a mischievous face at Jonah and said, "Okay, I can see why you want to get to know her story more."

Jonah rolled his eyes and replied with a smirk, "Well, sure. It is also that, along with the intrigue that I found her wandering and hiding in the auction venue."

Just then, Najib came up to Nevada and greeted her at a distance. They were both introduced formally, and then Jonah told her that this was the time that they would now be leaving for the airport. Jonah and Najib said their final goodbyes as they hugged for the last time.

***

"Okay, here we go." Upon entering the airport ground, the driver took them to the far end, where there was a small plane waiting. Jonah thanked the driver as they got out of the car and boarded the plane. A man sitting a few rows behind them silently was one of the security people that was to keep Jonah safe. It was Hakim. The man who once stayed with Jonah at the safe house. He got up, greeted Jonah, and then went right back to his assigned seat in the back while keeping a close eye on Nevada. Jonah knew that this was Najib's doing to keep him safe and keep Najib at peace.

"So, will you tell me where we are going though, Jonah?" Nevada asked.

"Someplace safe," Jonah replied. "I know that we do not know much about each other. I have a private room for you, and you can stay if you want. How does that sound?"

Nevada finally relaxed and felt amazingly comfortable. After the plane left the airfield, Jonah said, "I must close my eyes and try to catch some sleep if you don't mind. Don't worry. See the guy back there? He is just going to watch you until we land while I sleep. Just relax, and we will be okay. After all, I don't want you to kill me."

Jonah snickered and then shut his eyes.

***

When Jonah returned home, he had to push the front door due to the pile of mail that was pushed through the mail slot. He was not paying much attention to the lot. *"I am exhausted from the trip, so I am probably going to sleep tonight. We can have a proper talk in the morning,"* Jonah said to Nevada. *"Please feel free to do the same and freshen up if you'd like."*

Jonah went up to Hakim and told him that there was a room right next to his that he was planning to turn into an arsenal. But now that Hakim would be staying with him till further notice, he could take that one.

Nevada, on the other hand, took the room down the hall as it looked over the farm. Unbeknownst to Jonah, Nevada could think of her home while looking at the view. That was the only positive thing she could think of when she thought of home, and Jonah was about to find out a lot more in a lot less time. For now, all the three of them could consider doing was sleeping after a long and tiring journey back home to Hays, Kansas, a home that Jonah always found safe and a place to rest.

Made in the USA
Las Vegas, NV
05 June 2023

72938062R00105